BALANCE OF POWER
A DCI PILGRIM CRIME THRILLER
BOOK 6

By
A L Fraine

The book is Copyright © to Andrew Dobell, Creative Edge Studios Ltd, 2019.
No part of this book may be reproduced without prior permission of the copyright holder.

All locations, events, and characters within this book are either fictitious, or have been fictionalised for the purposes of this book.

Book List

www.alfraineauthor.co.uk/books

Acknowledgements

Thank you to my wife Louise for her tireless support, my kids for being amazing, and my family for believing in me.

Thank you to my amazing editor Crystal Wren for her critical eye and suggestions, they're always on point.

Thank you to my fellow authors for their continued inspiration.

And finally, thank you to you, the readers, for reading my crazy stories.

Table of Contents

Book List 2
Acknowledgements 2
Table of Contents 3
1 4
2 16
3 32
4 39
5 54
6 67
7 80
8 92
9 101
10 111
11 121
12 135
13 148
14 159
15 174
16 185
17 195
18 203
19 210
20 221
21 234
22 243
23 251
24 259
25 273
26 290
Author Note 303

1

Jess's phone beeped and buzzed, making her jump. It snapped her out of the daydream she'd been lost in as she mindlessly watched another episode of Rich House, Poor House.

It was one of those programmes she just couldn't help but get lost in. It was like an addiction, one that could be both life-affirming and aspirational. Although, if she wasn't in a good mood, it could send her spiralling into a grumpy stupor as she remembered her old life. The weekly struggle of not having enough money. The bare cupboards, the ever-present hunger, and the arguments. That was always the worst part. Back before her mother disappeared, when things had been really bad and they were forever getting at one another, it was like living in a warzone.

But she was out of all that now. Away from her father's dodgy dealings and her brother's troublemaking, but most of all, away from their rude, disgusting comments about how she made a living.

Jess shook her head to clear those thoughts from her mind and picked up her phone. There were a couple of alerts waiting for her, a message from a friend, and a notification from HoundPic.

She could guess who that was.

Opening the text from her friend, Lisa, she read it silently as the TV played to its audience of one in the background.

"When are we hitting the town again, J?" It read. "I wanna see if I can find that guy."

Jess raised an eyebrow at her friend's message and tapped in her reply. "Which one, the ginger one, or the bald one?"

A shrug emoji appeared in reply. "Either."

"Whore." Jess answered and chuckled to herself.

"I know, right?"

"I guess I've not got much room to talk, though." Jess answered, adding some laughing emojis at the end.

While she waited for Lisa to text again, she navigated over to the HoundPic app and opened it. Her feed appeared on the screen, displaying the images from the other profiles she followed. She tapped on the icon on the top right. Her profile appeared, along with her bio and thumbnails of her images. She briefly scrolled over the recent images of herself that she'd posted, passing a critical eye over them, spotting things she'd do differently before she entered the messages section. There'd been a few new ones come in, and they seemed to be the usual comments.

Declarations of love, compliments on her appearance, suggestions about what she should post next, and the inevitable smattering of sexual suggestions that came with the territory of doing what she did.

She didn't care much. They were paying subscribers, they paid to see her sexy pictures, and they paid well, which in turn paid for her house, food and bills.

At the top was another new message from Wyndy.

She opened it.

"Hiya. How are you tonight? What are you doing? Not watching more Rich House, Poor House, are you?"

For a brief moment, Jess panicked as she wondered how he knew. But, the answer was obvious. They'd talked about this before and her addiction to that particular programme. Like her, Ken 'Wyndy' Wyndam enjoyed the programme, especially the part when the rich family helped the poor one at the end.

She returned her attention to the message.

"It'll rot your brain, you know, watching that. Trust me, I know from experience."

Wink emoji.

She started typing her reply. "You've got a partially rotted brain? That's probably why you pay money to see photos of my ass." She always enjoyed needling him with sarcastic comments and seeing how far she could push him. He deserved it after that stunt he'd pulled on her a few weeks ago.

Her chest tightened as she remembered that day. She had vivid memories of opening her front door to find one of her fans on her doorstep. It was a moment of pure terror, realising that this middle-aged man knew where she lived. She still didn't quite know how he found her address, but she believed she handled it well.

Hell, he'd promised never to return, which was something at least. He'd upped his subscription, buying several more sets of images and video from her in the weeks since, no doubt as a way of saying sorry.

And frankly, as far as she was concerned, that was the very least he could do. She intended to fleece him for as much as she could get while being something of a bitch to him in the meantime.

Screw him.

A thud came from upstairs.

Jess froze.

She looked at the ceiling, her ears pricked up, straining to pick out any other sounds. Was it next door? They did bang on the wall occasionally.

It just didn't sound like it was… was it?

It was probably nothing, and after a moment, the phone buzzed in her hand again.

"I do that because you're beautiful, you know that."

Jess rolled her eyes at his fawning comments and sighed, almost feeling sorry for him.

"Thank you." She typed, unable to bring herself to be mean or sarcastic again. "What are you doing tonight?"

"Not a lot."

There was another thud.

Jess's heart leapt as she grabbed the remote and muted the TV.

Half out of her seat, her body tense, she gazed at the ceiling again, as if she could somehow see through it. That had to be in the house. It had to be.

Her phone buzzed.

"Just thinking of you." Wyndy's message read.

A shiver shot down her spine, and she closed the app. Getting to her feet, she turned to the TV and went to turn it off with the remote and then wondered if she was doing the right thing.

If there was someone in the house, they'd know she'd heard them.

"Shit," she hissed to herself under her breath.

Maybe she was imagining things? What were the chances of someone actually breaking into an upstairs window? Slim, surely, and yet there was a creeping kind of presence in the air, and she didn't feel alone anymore.

It was at moments like this that she wished she had a dog.

But, what should she do?

Scenes from countless horror films flashed before her eyes. Images of the silly blonde girl who goes to investigate the strange noise alone, without any kind of weapon.

She did not want to be that girl.

Picking up her phone, she called Conrad. She hated when he was at work, and she was home alone. She earned enough for both of them to live on, so why did he feel the need to work as well?

It was silly.

But the call didn't even connect, meaning his phone was off. She was about to hang up before the answerphone asked her to leave a message.

She briefly considered not bothering before changing her mind.

"Conrad. I'm err..." The house remained silent all around her. She'd not heard another creak or thud since the second one. "I'm probably being silly, but I just thought there might be someone in the house with me, and I got a little worried and... I don't know. It's probably nothing. I'll see you when you're back, okay?"

She hung up and sighed, feeling a little calmer after leaving the message. For a moment, she briefly considered sitting back down and chalking the noises up to the neighbours, but there was still a little nagging worry that played at the corner of her mind.

She called Lisa.

"Hey Jess," Lisa said, answering the phone quickly. "Sorry, I was about to reply…"

"Lisa… I think… I think there's someone in the house… maybe…"

"Maybe?"

"I heard bangs, like, thuds. I don't know. It could be the neighbours. Maybe I'm hearing things."

"And maybe you're not," Lisa suggested, setting Jess's heart racing again. "If you think there's someone in there with you, then you need to get out. Don't be silly, Jess. Don't be an idiot."

"I… I know."

"Where are you?"

"In my front room."

"Shut the door, at least. You could barricade it?"

Jess glanced down at the sofa. "I… guess I could."

"So, you just heard two thuds, is that it?"

"Yeah."

"And you're sure they came from inside your house?"

"I err… Maybe?"

"Is there anyone you can call? Where's Conrad?"

"He's at work, so his phone's off." Jess sighed.

"Aaah. What about a neighbour? Can you ask one to come around?"

"Um, yeah. If they're in."

"It's nearly midnight, Jess. They'll be in."

"But, I might wake them up."

"And you might get killed tonight."

"Don't say that." Jess grimaced at the thought. "I bet it's all in my imagination."

"And what if it isn't, hmmm?" Lisa suggested. "I don't want to see you on the news tomorrow."

Jess took a long deep breath and let it out slowly before walking towards the open lounge door. Taking a step into the hall with her phone still at her ear, she looked left, up the stairs.

She couldn't see or hear anything, and yet, there was something... Something was clawing at her mind.

"Jess, what are you doing?"

"I'm looking up the stairs."

"Do not go up there, you silly mare. Get out the house."

Jess nodded and backed towards the front door. She turned, realising she'd not looked in that direction and saw... just her front door.

"I'm stepping out now," she said and unlocked it, half expecting something to come shooting out of the shadows at the last moment and grab her.

She opened the door and glanced back, with a crawling feeling up her spine.

But the hallway was empty as she stepped out into the cold.

The street outside was dark, lit by the bright glow of LED streetlamps. Cars passed by, the occasional pedestrian could be seen further up.

Normal. Everything was unnervingly normal.

"Are you outside?"

"Yeah... It's cold."

"But you're safe."

"I guess."

"Go and knock on your neighbour's door."

"I can't do that. They'll think I'm crazy, or even more crazy than they already think I am."

"Who gives a shit? That doesn't matter. What matters is making sure there's no one in your house."

Jess sighed and looked back into her hallway. It was quiet and still.

Normal.

Warm.

Inviting.

She heard footsteps and turned to see a woman walk past on the street, giving her a strange look.

Jess screwed her face up, realising she was standing outside in her jogger bottoms, vest top, and big fluffy Pokemon slippers. She looked a sight.

"I might go back in. This is silly. It's probably nothing."

"No, Jess. Don't you dare."

"There's no one in my house. It was probably just the house settling or a pipe popping."

"And if it's not?"

"I'll get a knife, from the kitchen."

"Jess!"

"I'll call you back," Jess said and ended the call. Turning back to her house, she paused on the threshold before steeling herself and walking back inside.

Get a grip, Jess!

She closed the door behind her and shivered the last of the cold air away as the warmth of the house wrapped around her, comforting her. Looking up the stairs again, she shook her head at her paranoia. There wasn't anyone in the house, and the noises she'd heard, were most likely the neighbours or something.

Taking a few steadying breaths, she walked into the kitchen and pulled the biggest knife she had out of the knife block on the countertop before walking back to the front room. Still, she saw nothing. She moved back into the living room and returned to her programme, with the knife on the chair arm beside her, just in case.

Her phone buzzed repeatedly until she grabbed it, scanned through the string of messages from Lisa, and sent a quick reply to say all was fine. Her phone fell silent after that, allowing her to get comfortable and finally relax.

Restarting the programme, she turned the volume down and watched the last twenty minutes as fatigue crept up on her.

As the programme finished, she found herself drifting off to sleep and forced herself to get up. She wandered upstairs, only remembering the knife she'd left on the sofa once she was already half undressed.

For a brief moment, she considered going to get it before telling herself to stop being silly and get to bed. Conrad would be back before she knew it, and all would be fine.

Something caught her eye to her right.

She turned, looked, and saw a figure in the darkness striding towards her bedroom. She couldn't make out any details or see who it was in the shadows of her landing.

Several thoughts crashed through her head in the space of a second. Was that her boyfriend? What was Conrad doing home this early? Why hadn't she heard him come in? What was he doing? Was that Conrad? Maybe it wasn't. Maybe it was someone else.

Why was he carrying a knife?

A moment later, she saw his face, and then the screaming started.

2

Sitting on the edge of his bed in the darkness of the early hours, Jon ended the call by tapping the icon on his mobile. The screen bathed him in a cool glow, making him squint before he turned his phone away.

"We've been called in, right?"

Jon sighed and turned to look over his shoulder at the woman in his bed. Kate raised her eyebrows to emphasise the question.

"Aye, we have."

"Ugh, wonderful," she said, and with a grunt, sat up. She yawned and ran her hand over her face and through her hair. "What time is it?"

Jon checked the screen of his phone. "Four in the morning."

"Can't they get anyone else?"

"Apparently not, and this is in our wheelhouse."

"Shit. It's probably a bad one, then."

"I think so. A young woman's been murdered."

"Fuck. It's always women."

"Mmm," Jon grunted, agreeing with her. It always was, and it was usually always men doing the killing, too. He sighed, exasperated by the familiar but grotesque pattern.

"I'm going to jump in the shower. I'll be out in five," Kate said, jumping out of bed and grabbing her clothes.

Jon gave his head a shake and focused on the job at hand. "I'll get dressed and sort out some toast," he called out.

"Perfect," she answered from the bathroom before shutting the door behind her. Seconds later, he heard the shower start.

A selfish part of him wanted to wander in there and join her in the shower, but instead, he got up and got dressed. He was soon downstairs waiting beside the toaster as it slowly singed two slices of bread when he heard Kate exit the shower.

Minutes later, she wandered into the kitchen, preceded by a waft of her deodorant that he briefly enjoyed while buttering the toast.

Kate finished tying her hair up and grabbed the first slice. "Thanks." She took a bite with a crunch.

"Pleasure," he replied and picked up his own as he pulled his keys out and jingled them at her. "Ready?"

"I guess so. Let's go fight some crime."

Jon laughed.

"How Bruce Wayne stays up all night in those films, I'll never know. I need my sleep. Clearly, he's just weird."

"Yeah, it's the sleeping during the day that makes him weird, not the dressing up as a six-foot-bat, thing."

She elbowed him. "Shut it, you. You can drive, by the way."

"Thank you so much," Jon said as they walked out of the house.

"You staying over certainly makes these early morning call-ins easier," Jon remarked as they climbed into his car and pulled away.

"Yeah, it's nice, spending time at yours. My place is so small," she lamented.

"Your place is cute and very you."

"Thanks. I like your house better, though. Maybe I should move in?"

"Huh?"

Kate snorted. "The look on your face."

"Oh, sorry," Jon said, suddenly self-conscious about what face he'd pulled. He couldn't really remember and wondered if he's looked shocked or surprised or something. He hoped she wouldn't get offended.

"It's all right," she said, still giggling.

Was she being serious? Surely, she was joking... He frowned and wondered why he felt so surprised by her suggestion? It had come out of the blue, for sure, but they'd been steady as a couple for a while now, so it wasn't as if it was totally unexpected, and he did love having her to stay.

But having her move in with him sounded like a big step, and the last person he'd lived with was his last girlfriend before she was cruelly taken from him.

Murdered.

Was he tempting fate by having Kate move in? It had been five years ago, and yet, that was no time at all.

Jon sucked in a long breath and held it, before letting it go slowly. He didn't know how to deal with that.

"It's Ellie's first day, today," Kate said, changing the subject. Her comment snapped Jon out of his thoughts and brought his attention back to the here and now.

"Oh yeah. I'd forgotten about that. Do you think she'll be a good fit?"

"I think so," Kate said.

"Me too. She worked really well with us on that other case."

"She did. Did you have any thoughts about what you'll set her doing?"

"Depends on what comes in," Jon remarked with a shrug.

"How about partnering her with Nathan?"

Jon raised his eyebrows. "Nathan?"

"Yeah."

"Why?"

"Tradition," Kate answered. "Back when we were the Surrey Murder Team, and Nathan was still persona non-grata, newbies were always partnered with him. It was a kind of hazing ritual."

"I remember you telling me about that."

"It worked out for me."

Jon chuckled. "I guess so." He gave it a moment's thought before giving her a shrug. "I don't see why not. Can't do any harm."

"Exactly. Besides, it might put a smile on Nathan's grumpy face."

"You never know your luck. Alright, Nathan, it is then."

"Perfect."

"Wonderful," Jon said, as they rounded a corner and brought the all too familiar circus of blue lights and police cars that attended a major crime scene into view. "Here we go again."

"Don't sound too enthused, whatever you do," Kate remarked from the passenger seat. "You might blow a gasket."

"You're bright and breezy today? What's got into you?"

"Dunno. Maybe it's the thrill of the hunt?"

"Mmm. Well, if this is as bad as I think it'll be, trust me, there's nothing to get excited about."

"I know. I'm just wide awake and ready to get to work."

"Ten minutes ago, you didn't know how Batman did it, and now you sound like Batgirl, ready to take on Harley Quinn."

"You know your comic book characters," she stated, sounding surprised.

"I've seen some of the films."

"I never took you for a geek."

"Geek is the new black these days," he defended himself with a raised eyebrow.

"It certainly is. So, I'm Batgirl to your Batman, is that it?"

"I guess. Or are you Catwoman?"

"Pfft, you just want to see me in a catsuit."

"I'm saying nothing," Jon replied. "I'll just get myself into trouble."

"Aaah, well. I won't bother then. I mean, I was going to indulge you, but seeing as you're not interested…"

"Aaah, no, I didn't say that."

"No, no, no. It's fine. I'll cancel my order for the catsuit. No problem. Besides, I think we need your head in the game for this one."

"Yeah," Jon agreed as he pulled up close to the police line and gazed out at the madness that was engulfing this quiet Guildford Street. "I think we're in for a long day."

Kate followed his gaze. "Yeah, looks that way. Come on."

Jon climbed out of the car and spoke to the duty officer, who confirmed their identities before letting them through, logging their entry.

The street was no different to hundreds of others around the county. A usually quiet, residential affair, with cars parked up along the road, and townhouses lining the street on either side.

Local residents, disturbed by the commotion, were already out in the street, watching the hubbub. Some were still dressed in pyjamas and dressing gowns, their arms crossed against the cold as they talked amongst themselves. He spotted a few members of the press who'd arrived early too, no doubt putting in the overtime.

The street wasn't too far out from the city, and the house at the centre of the cordon was a three-story terrace townhouse, lit up by work lights and the strobing blue from the police vehicles.

"Evening, detectives. Did we get you out of bed?" Sergeant Dyson asked as he wandered over on seeing their approach.

"You did," Jon answered, his tone flat.

"Well, don't expect to get back there any time soon. This one's a doozy. You'll need to suit up before you go in there." Dyson motioned to the back of a nearby van, where he and

Kate slipped on the white forensic coveralls that were provided to them.

"Looks like you're getting me into an all-in-one, after all," Kate snarked.

"Not quite what I had in mind," Jon quipped back before looking over at Dyson. "So, what are we dealing with here?"

"Just one victim. A woman who looks like she's barely twenty, at a guess. Whoever did this went to town on her. She's a mess."

"It's a bad one, then?" Kate asked.

"Not for the faint-hearted, no. I don't often see them this bad," Dyson confirmed.

Jon watched a man in a forensics suit exit the house, sit down, and pull his mask off before burying his head in his hands as he got some air.

Jesus, it must be bad.

"Who called us in?" Kate asked.

"A neighbour heard screaming and called the police. An officer attended, found the back door open, and investigated."

They finished up, and Jon started to make for the house. "You coming in?" Jon asked Dyson.

"Nope. I've been in. I don't want to see that again unless I have to."

Jon pulled a face and looked over at Kate. She bugged her eyes at him before he set off and made for the house again. They passed several more forensics officers on their way in.

Jon spotted Sheridan, the Crime Scene Manager, in a similar white suit, in the hallway just beyond the front door, talking with another officer.

She turned towards them as they entered. "Jon, Kate. Thanks for coming."

"Wouldn't miss this for the world," Kate said.

"You might regret those words," Sheridan said. "Did Dyson give you the rundown?"

"Only briefly. Female victim and it sounds like it'll be a gory one."

"You could say that," Sheridan confirmed. "You'd better come and see."

Jon looked around as they followed Sheridan, checking the side rooms of the lounge and kitchen with a glance before making their way upstairs.

"Nice place," Jon remarked.

"It is," Sheridan confirmed. "Very nice."

"She must have been making bank," Kate added. "Lot's of space."

"Any idea who she was?"

"We have a name based on her ID," Sheridan said. "Jessica Thornton."

"Good, thanks. Anyone else in the house?"

"No one, no. The Medical Examiner's been and gone. Not too much for him to do. She's certainly dead."

Jon grimaced as Sheridan led them across the first-floor landing towards a side door and stopped just outside.

"Ready?" Sheridan asked.

Jon could already see blood splatter from his vantage point and took a brief moment to steel his nerves and detach himself from his emotions before he nodded, and Sheridan led them in. He needed to be cold and analytical about this, and look for clues rather than empathise too much with the victim. If he didn't, it might all become too much, and he'd need to get some air himself.

The girl lay spread-eagled on the bed, naked and butchered. Blood was everywhere. It was as if the killer had been throwing it around the room. The smell was overpowering.

"OK," he said, keeping his breath steady. "What do you know."

Sheridan moved closer to the bed. "The killer used a sharp implement, a knife most likely, and he focused on several key areas when he attacked her. Her groin, breasts, and face, stabbing her multiple times, and cutting her face up."

"It's like he was attacking what made her female," Jon remarked.

"Are her breasts... gone?" Kate asked, frowning at the scene.

"They were cut off, yes. We've found them, in bits, discarded around the room." She pointed at a few places where numbered markers stood next to gory viscera.

Even though he managed to stay mostly detached, Jon couldn't help but feel sick as he gazed over the scene. It was horrific, and he couldn't help but feel for the poor victim. "Was she alive when he did this?" He almost didn't want to know the answer.

"If it is a 'he'," Kate said.

"It probably is," Jon replied. "But yeah, point taken."

"For some of it, I think so. The blood splatter is indicative of a struggle. Also, the screaming the neighbour heard. It suggests she tried to fight back."

"Not that it did her any good," Kate remarked.

"No, it did not."

"Anything else? A murder weapon? DNA? Any other clues?"

"No weapon, no. We'll see what we can find otherwise, but DNA and such takes time, as you know."

"Of course," Jon replied.

"We think we have an ingress point though," Sheridan said. "It looks like the killer climbed into the back garden, up onto the roof of the extension outback, and then got in through a window. We're dusting for prints, but there's none so far."

"So, they sneaked in and waited upstairs for her?"

"It looks that way. He could have been waiting in the house for hours, for all we know."

"Okay, thank you," Jon said, as he heard shouting coming from outside, and the sounds of a struggle.

"You hear that?" Kate asked.

"I do," Jon replied and left the room with Kate on his heels as more shouts reached his ears.

Outside, on the front lawn, he saw a young man on his knees, being held by a couple of uniformed officers.

"Let me go," the detainee yelled. "I need to see her. Let go of me. You can't do this."

"Who's this?" Jon asked as he removed his face covering.

"Claims to be the boyfriend," one of the officers said. "Made a break for the house."

Jon nodded and regarded the young man. He had tears in his eyes, and his face was contorted in fury as he fought against the grip of the policemen. Jon crouched before him and met his eyes. "Hi, I'm Detective Pilgrim, and this is Detective O'Connell."

"Hi," she said.

"Are you Jessica's partner?"

"Yes, ugh." He struggled again.

"If you're going to be unreasonable, they won't let you go," he stated.

"What's going on? Why are you here? Is Jess okay? Why won't anyone talk to me?"

Jon sighed. "Son, please, you need to calm down. We'll tell you everything, but you need to do as we ask."

"Jess. Is Jess okay? Has someone hurt her?"

He needed to know, it was his right, and it might just calm him down. "I'm sorry, but no. Jess isn't okay. She's... gone."

"What?" He whimpered. "No. She can't be. She was here when I left."

"I'm sorry," Jon said, noting how the young man seemed to sag in the grip of the officers, his strength draining from him.

"Oh god. You mean... she's dead?"

"That's right, I'm sorry."

"Did someone... I mean..." Tears were streaming down his face as he struggled to find the words. "Was she..."

"We think she was attacked," Kate said. "It certainly looks that way."

The young man buried his head in his hands and cried as the officers let him go at Jon's nod. He placed his hand on the man's back to comfort him, as he slowly got his emotions under control.

"No, no, no," he muttered between sobs, denying the reality of what had happened. "But, she called me," he said eventually.

"Called you?" Jon asked.

"My phone was off. She left a message saying she thought someone was in the house with her. I got the message as soon as I finished work, so I rushed over."

"We're going to need to hear that message," Jon said.

He nodded.

"What's your name?" Kate asked.

"Conrad. Conrad Horton," the young man replied, his voice cracking from the emotions that were coursing through him.

"I'm sorry for your loss, Conrad," Jon said, as images of the dead girl flashed in his mind. He knew how this felt and sympathised with him and what he was going through. He'd have some tough days ahead, not least of which would be the interviews he'd need to give to him and Kate. "But, we're going to need to speak to you, and you can't go into the house right now. It's a crime scene. You understand?"

"I think so. I just... I wanted to see her."

"You don't want to see her," Kate said. "Not like this. She wouldn't want you to, trust me."

"My colleague is right, believe me. You don't want that as your last memory of her." Images of the girl mixed with images of Jon's former girlfriend as he remembered being the one to find her after her murder.

Those images would live with him forever and haunted his nightmares. He wanted to save Conrad from suffering the same fate.

Conrad went to protest, but the words wouldn't come and died on his lips as he sagged once more. "No, you're right. I wouldn't want to see that."

"Good lad," Jon said. "Do you think you could answer some questions?"

He nodded and then looked up suddenly, with fire in his eyes. "It's her dad, or brother, or both."

"What?" Jon asked.

"They killed her."

Jon raised a hand. "Now, just hold on a moment. We'll get to that. I think we need to get you out of here, first, okay?"

"Oh, sure. Okay," Conrad said, his head sagged as he deflated.

"Hold onto those thoughts, and we'll talk soon."

He bit his lip and gave Jon a nod.

"Good." As he watched the officers walk Conrad away, Jon turned to Kate. "He's already placing blame."

"On her dad and brother," Kate said.

"Mmm. I have a feeling this is going to be an interesting one."

3

"I like it, it's got great prospects for growth, and I think it could do well for us," Elden said, taking another glance over the accounts and projected figures that were displayed on his laptop.

The small startup had done well in its first year of business, growing faster than its owners had anticipated, but there was still so much further it could go. But it was hampered by the usual things, a lack of funds to really push it, and a dearth of good contacts within the industry itself.

Luckily for them, this was something that Elden and his team specialised in, and the startup was more than happy for them to come on board as partners and give them what they needed to go stratospheric.

"So, you want to go for it?" the voice on the other end of the line asked. "You want me to make the transfer?"

"Do it," Elden replied. "Tell them the champagne is on me."

"Yes, sir, and sorry for the early call."

"No problem, this needed doing. Good work. We'll talk later." Elden hung up the phone.

Sitting back in his soft leather office chair, he yawned. His team had been working through the night, running the numbers and negotiating with the directors of the startup, but now was the time to bite the bullet.

Today might be a good day, after all.

He took a long relaxing breath and contemplated returning to bed, but he was up now, so what was the point? He had a busy day ahead of him, no doubt, dealing with the aftermath of this latest deal, as well as his weekly visit to the prison to see Solomon.

Staring at the displayed photos that featured his son's smiling face, he sighed and rolled his eyes. Despite his best efforts and as much money as he could throw it the problem, Solomon remained locked up.

Since then, and following the events at the mansion with Abban, things with the organisation had gone quiet. It wasn't very surprising, after how brazen they had become. Too brazen, really. They had attracted too much of the wrong kind of attention, so they needed to sink back into the shadows and allow the ripples to die away.

"Hey, sweetie, you coming back to bed?"

Elden looked up at Gabrielle in the door to his office. "Maybe," he lied.

"Good, because, I miss you..." She slowly pulled the shoulder of her robe down, revealing a breast. "I need someone to keep me warm."

Elden sighed and didn't care if she noticed his reaction. She was the latest in a string of short-lived flings he'd indulged in with young women, preferring not to get too tied down, but sometimes he just wanted to be left alone.

"Sure, sure. I'll be back up soon." Could she make out the 'get lost' message, written between the lines?

"Don't be too long," she answered, undoing the robe completely and allowing it to fall open, showing him everything.

She was attractive. There was no denying that, but his mind was elsewhere, and he wasn't sure he wanted to jump back into bed with her right now.

"No, I won't," he said and rubbed the bridge of his nose as he felt the beginning of a headache brewing. As he opened his eyes again, he noticed a blinking red light in the corner of the laptop screen. He frowned at it and picked up his phone, which had been face down on the desk.

There was an alert on it.

Security breach.

Elden frowned. Had he missed this? How long ago did this happen?

The muscles of his chest tightened as his heart rate spiked. What was going on?

There was an almighty bang from the front hallway just outside his office and a yelp of surprise from Gabrielle.

What the hell? Where was his security?

Elden got up and strode around his desk, making it halfway across his office before he saw a figure in black step up to Gabrielle as she hugged her robe close.

The dark figure raised his arm. He was carrying a gun and proceeded to shoot Gabrielle in the head without hesitation.

She crumpled to the floor, lifeless, as a much larger figure walked into view. He stopped a short distance from the office, locking eyes with Elden.

The bald head and severe expression were unmistakable.

"Terry," Elden gasped in barely contained shock as the man gave him a lopsided smile.

Balling his fists, Elden's mind raced as he considered his options. He knew of only one reason why Terry would be in his house.

After he took the fall for Abban, only for him to end up in jail anyway, the rumours that had come out of High Down Prison were clear and somewhat concerning.

Terry wanted revenge.

The group's leaders had rationalised that he only wanted revenge on Abban, and had got it. So maybe he was mollified. Privately, Elden had not been so sure, but there was little evidence to suggest Terry wanted revenge on the whole group, until now.

Taking a step back, he moved away from the large man. He needed to warn the others. Their contact with each other had been sporadic at best, so they might not know about Terry for days if he didn't warn them somehow. But how?

He needed options and time to do what he needed, but he was at a distinct disadvantage and had been caught off guard. His mind went to what weapons he might have or be able to get to help defend himself or even fight back.

He had a couple of guns on the property. His hunting rifle in the outhouse and an unregistered pistol in a lockbox in another room. Elden screwed his face up at the thought. Could he even remember the code to get to it? Probably not.

Well, that wouldn't do him much good, would it?

"Elden," Terry rumbled as he approached the office door, blocking the only exit. "That your girl?"

"I guess," Elden admitted and glanced at Gabrielle's vacant face on the hall floor as blood soaked into her hair. He'd only known her a few weeks, and she'd already started to annoy him. He didn't mourn her, but despite him doing some horrific things in his life, she didn't deserve to be killed just for being in this house.

"Shame."

"I didn't know you cared," Elden said, wanting to keep Terry talking and stave off the inevitable.

"I don't."

"So, is this it then? Are you coming for all of us?"

Terry smiled and raised the gun he was holding.

"No, please, wait," Elden cried, raising his hands and screwing his eyes shut as he waited for whatever came next. Would it hurt? Would Terry try to kill him outright or make him suffer? "Don't."

He waited, his muscles tense, but when the bullet didn't come, Elden eased one eye open. Terry was still there, and so was the gun.

"Why not?"

"I... I could offer you... something?"

"Do you realise how pathetic you are, Mr Lichwood, now the power has been stripped from you, now that I hold your life in my hands. Just look at you. Look how you grovel before me, and beg for your life. I bet you'd give me anything just to keep me from pulling this trigger, right?"

"Anything, just name it," Elden answered without even thinking about it. It was true, he would hand over anything and everything to keep on living. He actually shocked himself when he came to that realisation and almost couldn't believe it.

"Every penny you own."

"Done," Elden replied, clutching at straws. Besides, he thought, he felt sure there'd be a way for him to get it back, and even take his revenge on this brute later.

Terry laughed. It was a deep, full sound, almost like a bark. "You're fucking pathetic, you know that? Do you think I'd let you live after this? Do you think I'd just take payment from you and walk away? You'd find a way to screw me over, wouldn't you?"

"No!" He was lying and knew it deep down, but he couldn't say that, not if he wanted to live.

Terry gave his head a long slow shake.

"I'm not lying. I wouldn't breathe a word of this to anyone else. I promise."

"Like I said, pathetic. Truly, pathetic."

Terry's arm tensed. There was an ear-shattering noise, and then nothing.

4

"Aww, the day's barely started, and it already feels like the evening," Jon said as he walked into the main operations room at Horsley Station. It was early, and the sky outside remained a dim slate grey, shot through with slowly brightening blue as the sun started to rise on another day in Surrey.

"I know what you mean," Kate agreed. "Coffee?"

"Aye, why not. It might wake me up," Jon replied with a sigh and then stopped short as he turned back to her. "I've never asked, but do you put the milk in first in coffee too? Or is it just tea that you subject to your fiendish ways?"

Kate smiled back at him. "The tea witch never gives up her secrets."

She walked away.

Jon rolled his eyes as he looked across the room, pleased to see there were plenty of people already in. It seemed like he and Kate weren't the only ones who'd been called in early.

Wandering to his right, Jon entered his office and set his things down before powering up the PC and logging in. He rubbed his hands over his face, as he waited for the machine to boot up, preparing himself until Kate ambled back in carrying two mugs of steaming dark liquid.

The aroma of the beans filled his nose. He breathed it in, savouring the silky-smooth smell.

"I think we're going to need a few of these today," Kate commented.

"Aye. Tomorrow too, most likely, and the day after."

"I'll keep you topped up."

"Good, I don't think I'll get through this without my addictive heart attack fuel. I take it Conrad is in the building?"

"As far as I know," Kate replied. "I'll check up on that shortly."

"Good. We need to talk to him and find out what he knows."

"By the way, I messaged Dion on the drive back here and got him to look into Jess's family. Hopefully, he'll have something for us by now."

Jon nodded. "Here's hoping. So, what did you think of Conrad? Did he have something to do with this?"

"I don't know. It's hard to tell, but his reaction seemed genuine when he found out about her death."

"I thought the same," he admitted, thinking back. Watching the young man as he slumped into the damp grass, utterly defeated by the events of the morning, was heart-breaking. That kind of reaction was difficult to fake, but not impossible. They'd seen it done before, firsthand, so it paid never to take anything at face value.

"We'll look into him as well, see if he's got any skeles in his closest."

Jon nodded as Nathan walked up to the office door and knocked on the frame. A short woman with dark hair stood behind him.

"Jon," Nathan said with a return nod.

"Nathan."

"You had an early start, by the sound of things."

"Yep. They dragged us out of bed at some ungodly hour. I might have to make a statement to the criminal fraternity to stick to office hours, or something."

"Good luck with that," Nathan replied as he stepped into the room. The woman behind him followed and stepped out from behind him. "You remember Ellie?"

"How could I forget? How're things, DC Mizaki?"

"Good morning, sir. I'm well, thanks. Looking forward to today."

"Excellent, well, we'll see if you're still as excited after a day with these reprobates."

"I'm sure I will be, sir."

"Jon, call me Jon, please."

"Sorry, sir."

Jon gave her a look.

"I mean, Jon."

He gave her a curt nod. "We're pleased to have you here, Ellie, and frankly, it's about time. I think we're a little short-staffed, actually."

"Everywhere is, s... err, Jon."

"Ain't that the truth."

"DI Taylor said the same about me leaving his team, that they're going to be understaffed."

"So, he didn't like that you requested a transfer over here?" Kate asked.

"No, he did not," Ellie confirmed. "He had some err, choice words about it?"

"And about us, I bet," Kate added.

"Professional courtesy prevents me from saying any more," Ellie said, agreeing.

"I wouldn't expect anything less," Nathan said. "I was just on my way out and wondered what you wanted Ellie to do."

"I hear you were at a crime scene this morning," Ellie stated.

"We were. Murdered girl. The killer cut her up pretty bad. We have the boyfriend downstairs, who we're going to have a chat to, soon."

"I see."

Jon glanced at Nathan. "What have you got going on this morning?"

"Actually, I have my own crime scene to visit," Nathan replied and looked over at Kate. "It might interest you, actually."

"Oh?" Kate asked. "What is it?"

"You remember Elden Lichwood, right? Father of Solomon, the Urbex Killer?"

"Oh yes. I don't think I'll forget that one," Kate replied.

"What happened?" Ellie asked.

"The son of a wealthy businessman kidnapped several models after luring them to a fake photo shoot, then killed them inside a series of derelict buildings," Kate explained. "Nasty piece of work."

Ellie hissed in sympathy. "So, what does Urbex mean?"

"It's a portmanteau of two words. It means Urban Explorer," she explained.

"Those weirdos who think it's fun to break into derelict buildings and go exploring," Jon added.

"I see," Ellie replied.

"They're not weirdos," Kate countered. "I can see the beauty in such places."

"I bet you can," Jon said, and raised an eyebrow at her.

"Ignore him. He's northern," Kate said to Ellie.

"Aaah yes, I remember. It's the accent that gives him away."

"It's softening, though. We'll make him one of us before too long."

"Is it me, or does that sound desperately scary," Jon said to Nathan.

"Coming from Kate, with her Irish twang, it sounds mixed up."

Jon laughed, and put on his best approximation of an Irish accent. "To be sure, to be sure. Potatoes!"

"Thin ice Jon, thin ice," Kate said, a playful note of warning in her tone.

"Aye, whatever. Right then, Nathan, tell me more about this case. What's happened?"

"It seems like Mr Lichwood senior has been killed. I need to head on over there and check it out."

"Elden's been killed?" Kate asked. "Are you sure?"

"That's what the report said," Nathan confirmed.

"Shit."

Jon glanced between Kate and Nathan. "Do you want to go with him on this one?" He sensed there was a connection there for her and wondered if she wanted to follow it up.

"No," Kate replied after a moment's pause. "No, I don't think so. Nathan can handle it."

Nathan shrugged, choosing not to challenge or question her.

"Alright," Jon said, and returned his gaze to Nathan. "How about you take Ellie with you. She can be your partner on this one."

"Thank you, sir," Ellie replied.

"Sounds good to me," Nathan said, and looked over at Ellie. "You game?"

"Sounds good."

"Besides, it's tradition," Kate added.

"Aaah, I see what's going on here," Nathan said. "Going back to that, are we?"

"Her idea," Jon said, pointing at Kate and passing the blame.

"Of course, it was," Nathan answered. "It wouldn't be anyone else's."

"What's this all about?" Ellie asked.

"Don't worry about it. I'll tell you later," Nathan said with a sigh.

"And if mister grumpy pants doesn't tell you, I will," Kate added. "Come and find me later, if you like."

"I might do that anyway," Ellie replied. "Then we can have a chat without the boys."

"They're the best kind of chats," Kate agreed with a gleam in her eye.

"Alright, come on, let's go and see what happened to Mr Lichwood," Nathan said and made for the door. "I'll report back."

"Good, thanks, see you later," Jon replied, and watched them leave the room. He turned to Kate. "Are you sure you don't want to be a part of that investigation? You caught Elden's son, after all?"

"We did, but no. I don't think so," Kate said. "Thanks, though."

"That's okay. Just wanted to be sure."

"I know."

"Do you mind if I ask, why not?"

Kate screwed her face up and shrugged. "Um, I'm not sure, really. I guess it goes back to the whole Abban thing and that sick little organisation he was a part of. I'm fairly sure Elden was, too, although we had no evidence back then."

"Too many bad memories?" Jon asked, feeling sure he was starting to understand why she said no.

"Yeah, something like that. I just don't want to go anywhere near that if I can help it."

Kate's history with her former tormentor, Abban, who'd killed her aunt, was well known to Jon. The man had sent her letters and taunted her for years until he finally appeared from the shadows in one of the last cases she'd had with Nathan before Jon joined the team. They'd arrested him and sent him to prison for his crimes until he escaped and ended up being the focus of Jon's first case on the team.

He noticed Kate playing with her little finger, the one Abban had cut off before they'd managed to arrest him. The hospital had managed to reattach it, and she had regained most of the feeling and movement in it in the months since. But it was a constant reminder of what that depraved individual had done to her and how he'd affected her life.

He didn't blame her for wanting to keep well away from anything to do with that mess and started to wonder about Abban himself.

The last they'd heard, he'd been attacked in High Down Prison by Terry Sims before Terry had escaped and gone to ground. Abban had survived, but was severely injured during the assault.

Was he still alive? Had he recovered? Or had he finally left this mortal coil and freed Kate from the shadow he cast over her life? He might see about looking into all that if he found a moment later.

"Shall we see what Dion's got for us?" Kate was still holding her injured finger in her other hand. She put on a brave face, but he felt sure she was dealing with a few internal demons when it came to all this. Best to keep her distracted. Focus on the new case and keep her occupied.

"Sounds like a plan," Jon agreed and got up. He went to walk out of the office, only for her to reach out for him. He stopped, and she wrapped her arms around him and buried her face in his chest. He pulled her close and just held her for a moment but said nothing.

There was nothing to say, really. They both knew what this was about, and she just needed a moment's comfort.

He was happy to oblige.

Seconds later, she let go, and with a sniff, she looked into his eyes and gave him a weary smile. "Sorry."

"Don't be," he replied. "It's okay."

Recomposing herself she started for the door. "Shall we?"

They walked out of his office, across the open-plan work area, and found Dion sitting at his desk, with what looked like countless windows open on his screen. Beside him, Rachel was taking notes, and pointing to the screen.

They paused as Jon approached.

"Guv," Dion said. "Kate."

"Hey boss," Rachel added.

"Mornin' Dion, Rachel." Kate greeted them too. "So, what have you got for us?"

Dion sat back in his chair as Rachel made space for them.

"These early mornings, man," Dion said. "You're gonna kill me."

"Part and parcel of the job, you know that."

"I know that," Dion parroted back and yawned, stretching as he did it. "Right then, we've been looking into this Jessica Thornton, and well, she lives quite the life, it seems."

"How do you mean?"

"Well, she's quite prolific online. I've got her Twitter, Facebook, Instagram, Snapchat and TikTok accounts, and they all point to her HoundPic profile."

"HoundPic?" Jon asked. "What the hell's that?"

"It's one of these new fan or patron style sites, where creators can put up photos or art, and people pay subscriptions to get the content. HoundPic is that, but for people to post sexy pics."

"Porn?" Kate asked.

"Sometimes, but not always. There's cosplayers and models and even photographers on there, posting stuff from the shoots they do."

"Oh," Kate said. "So, what did Jess post?"

"Nudie stuff, I think, based on her Twitter feed. Softcore porn, basically. She posted some sneak peeks on her Twitter, like this." Dion brought up some examples showing Jess in various states of undress, wearing costumes or fancy underwear. It was all aimed at a very specific audience of men who liked that kind of thing, and she wasn't shy about showing herself off. Jon felt a little odd looking at these images, knowing she was now lying in the mortuary, butchered almost beyond recognition.

"Okay, thanks," Jon said, motioning to Dion that he should close the images on the screen. "So, she made a living off this?"

"Yes, and a good one, too. Look here. You can sign up to different levels of membership to her account. So, if we assume everyone's on the bottom tier, and times that by the number of subs she has…"

"Oh, wow. That's a couple of grand right there." Jon realised.

"And that's lowballing it," Dion stressed. "It's likely she was bringing in double or triple that from subs alone, not counting the stuff she sells outside of the subscriptions."

"Shit. No wonder she could afford that house."

"She was killing it," Kate agreed.

"It's a bit exploitative, though," Rachel said.

"How?" Kate asked. "No one was forcing her to post those pics. She's a good looking girl and saw a way to take advantage of men—and some women I guess—and make a damn good living for herself."

"Yeah, but it's not like it's a respectable way to make a living, is it? Catering to men's basic instincts."

Kate shrugged. "I doubt she cared. My guess is, she was laughing all the way to the bank."

"Until someone came calling for her," Dion said.

"One might have nothing to do with the other," Kate suggested.

"Maybe, maybe not."

"Alright," Jon said, cutting in, in an attempt to get them back on track, "so she was self-employed and making good money with her little homegrown business?"

"Correct," Dion said.

"And as we all know, a woman can't post anything online without a creep saying something gross, and given what she was posting, I think we can assume that she most likely had a few of them following her, maybe even subscribing to her. I wonder if any of these people were actual stalkers?"

Dion tapped a pen against his desk and continued, "I need access to her account."

"You do."

"Good thing I've already requested it then, isn't it?"

"Well done," Jon said with a wink. "I knew I kept you on the team for a reason."

"Conrad might know more about any stalkers," Kate suggested.

"He might, you're right. I assume Conrad knew about her business and what she was posting online?"

"Knew and approved, from what I can tell," Dion said and brought up another Twitter feed. "He was always retweeting her posts and sharing her stuff, so I think we can assume he was comfortable with her doing this."

"Okay, that's good," Jon said. "It means she wasn't hiding it from him, which means he's likely to know if there were any fans who got a little too close."

"We can only hope," Kate agreed.

"Okay, anything else?"

"Plenty," Dion answered. "Her family ties are certainly of interest. Both her brother Henry and her dad Mickey are known to us. They both have criminal records for violence and have ties to certain gangs and such too. Henry, or Henry as he's known in gangland," Dion snickered at his own joke, "his criminal activity is a little more recent, and we have reason to suspect he's actively involved in that kind of lifestyle still. The father is a labourer. An odd job man who goes from building site to building site, with a string of complaints following him. He's not been in trouble with us recently, though."

"Any mother on the scene?" Kate asked.

"No. Jess's mother's name is Cathy, but she disappeared six years ago. We have a missing person's case for her on the system, which we need to go through."

"Let's make that a priority. There might be something there," Jon said.

Dion made a note on his to-do list.

"Do we know what any of these family members thought of Jess, and what she did as a job?" Jon asked.

"Nope," Dion replied.

"I can think of one person in the building, who might know," Kate said.

Conrad, Jon thought, he might know. "Yeah, so can I."

"So, we have two suspects right away," Kate suggested as she glanced over at Jon.

"Seems that way," Jon replied. "It looks like Conrad was right to suspect her dad and brother."

5

Walking into the interview room, Jon was greeted by the sight of Conrad slumped over the table, his head resting on his arms, talking in low tones to the duty solicitor that had been assigned to him.

Conrad turned his head and looked up before closing his eyes and sighing loudly.

The solicitor urged him to sit up, which he did slowly and reluctantly as if his limbs were made of lead. He sat back and crossed his arms, appearing defensive and closed off as he watched Jon and Kate through red-rimmed eyes. He'd been crying, which was totally understandable, given the circumstances.

He wondered what the lawyer had been talking to him about. They'd likely warned him that this was not to be treated as a friendly chat or an interview. They were not meeting as equals here. No, he should treat this as an interrogation and not be too forthcoming about anything which might incriminate him.

Jon chewed his cheek as he mulled this over. It was true that Conrad was as much of a suspect as anyone else. After all, victims of murder were usually killed by someone who knew them. They were typically crimes of passion, and no one knew Jess better than he did, most likely.

But hopefully, for Conrad's sake, this young man was innocent and wanted to help. Jon had little doubt that things would become somewhat clearer once this interview, or interrogation, was over.

"Conrad, how are you holding up?" Jon asked.

He shrugged. "I've just found out my girlfriend has been murdered. How do you think I'm feeling?"

That was a little more defensive than he was expecting, but after a brief moment of feeling offended by Conrad's blunt reply, he reminded himself to cut the young man some slack. He was going through a horrific experience that few could really understand. In fact, he was one of the very few people who knew almost exactly what he was going through.

Jon gave him a solemn, understanding nod. "You're going through a lot, I understand."

"How can you possibly understand? How can you know what I'm feeling right now? Has your girlfriend been murdered by some psycho?"

"Actually, yes, she was, five years ago. And I was the one who found her," Jon replied, keeping his voice even. "So, I think I have an idea what you're going through."

Conrad's mouth worked silently for a moment, his jaw opening and closing as he searched for the right words. "Oh..." he said eventually. "I... didn't know."

"Of course you didn't. But that's okay. You know now, and believe me when I say, I want to help. We both do," he added, gesturing to Kate. "We've both lost people we care about and have some idea what it's like. We're here to help."

Conrad hung his head. He sniffed, and then wiped fresh tears from his eyes. "I just, I don't know what to do. I don't understand it. I can't believe she's gone, it doesn't... I don't..." He sobbed.

Jon slid a box of tissues over to him and gave him a moment to calm down. Conrad's head was almost certainly a riot of emotions and thoughts as he dealt with this heartbreaking situation. It would take time for him to figure things out and steady himself on these stormy waters.

He'd do what he could for the young man, and there was indeed help that they could recommend, but he couldn't let his sympathy for the man's situation take over. He had a job to do, and Jess was counting on him doing it.

Jess would want the killer brought to justice, no matter what.

Over the next few moments, Conrad managed to pull himself together enough that Jon felt able to continue with the interview process and went through the usual motions, setting the recorder going and introducing everyone for the benefit of the recorder.

"So, you're Jessica's boyfriend, right?" Jon asked.

"That's right."

"How long have you two been together?"

"Just over a year," he said. "I knew her for a month or so before we got together, but, yeah, a year, or thereabouts."

"And what do you do for a living?"

"I work in a warehouse, doing shift work. It's pretty boring, but it helps."

"Why would you do that?"

Conrad's eyebrows shot up, before he gave Jon a slight frown. "Why?"

"Yeah. Jess earned well. Very well, in fact. She probably didn't need your money, so why work?"

Conrad seemed a little shocked. "I didn't want to stop… Her money… well, it was a little volatile. Up and down, you know?"

"So, you were the safety net," Kate surmised.

"I err, yeah, I guess so." He shrugged. "We probably didn't need it, and if I'd given up earlier…" He teared up again and took a moment to get his emotions under control. He was clearly upset.

"Do you have family?"

"Yeah. They don't live around here, though."

"And where are they based?" Jon asked.

"Norfolk."

"On the other side of London," Kate said. "That's a fair old drive."

"I see them every so often," he muttered.

"Recently?"

"Not for a few months."

"Did they know about Jess's line of work?"

"No," he answered, looking a little uncomfortable. "They know she's a model, but that's all."

"But, she does more than that, doesn't she," Jon stated.

Conrad sighed, clearly understanding what Jon was getting at. "Yeah, she does."

"HoundPic," Kate said.

Conrad nodded.

"We're going to need to get into her profile," Jon said.

Conrad gave him a frown, looking a touch confused. "Why? What's this got to do with that? I told you who did it. It was her father or her brother. Hell, it was probably both. They hated her, and they hated me, too. They beat me up, you know? A few months ago, when they found out I was going to move in with her, they found me and attacked me."

"I'm sorry to hear that," Kate said.

"Did you report it?" Jon added.

"No. What's the point?" He sat back in a huff. "You wouldn't have done anything anyway. You never do."

"We do the best we can, under the circumstances," Jon answered.

"Yeah, meaning nothing, unless it's serious. Then all of a sudden, you're all over it, like flies on shit."

Jon bit his lip, realising that Conrad was in a delicate state and that challenging him on this would do no good. "You said they hated her."

"Yeah."

"Why?"

"Because of what she did. That's why. They hated that she earned as much money as she did, and they hated the way she did it."

"By using HoundPic?" Jon asked.

"That's right," he spat, sounding angry. "They've called her a slut and a whore more times than I can count. It's why she moved out."

"Okay, okay. Calm down, Mr Horton," Jon said, and raised a calming hand. "I want to understand this more. Can you help me? It might be important."

Conrad let out another sigh, and with his hands on the table, took a series of long, slow breaths. "Yeah, sure. What do you want to know?"

"Thank you, Conrad. So, take me back. How did she end up posting stuff to this website and getting hundreds of followers?"

"I think she started modelling in her teens when she was sixteen or something, you know. Doing fashion shoots and stuff. It was her mother who encouraged her to do it. I think someone approached her and asked if she'd do a shoot. Her mum went with her, and Jess loved it."

And her dad?" Jon asked, wanting to get as clear a picture as he possibly could.

"He didn't like it. Hated it, in fact, I think, but her mother encouraged her anyway and helped her. She went along to the shoots, too, to keep her dad off her back. It was like that for months, until her mother disappeared when she was about seventeen."

"What did Jess tell you about that and how it happened?"

"She told me that her mum and dad were arguing a lot, like, all the time. Things were bad between them for a while, and then one day, Jess woke up, and there was a note waiting for her from her mother, saying she had to leave and would be back to get her."

"And she never came back?" Kate asked.

"No, never."

"Why do you think that is?" Jon asked.

"Because he killed her, that's why. Jess's dad killed his wife, I'm sure of it. He's a murderer. He hated her. He hated what Jess was doing and that they were ignoring him, so he killed her and made Jess think that she'd run away. And now he's finally come after Jess too. It has to be."

"You said her brother, Henry, didn't like it either?"

"Henry, no. I think he was more embarrassed by it than anything else. He hated whenever it was brought up around him. He didn't want to be around that kind of talk at all. He didn't like his friends knowing either."

"In case they went looking for photos of her?"

Conrad shrugged. "Probably. She said he'd leave the room or shut down the conversation whenever it would come up. He just didn't want to hear about it."

"So, what happened next. You said her mother disappeared when Jess was seventeen, right?"

"That's right."

"So, what about Hound Pic, when did she start using that?"

"I think it was the next year, after she turned eighteen, that she started posting there. Some other models recommended it as a way to make more money. It was all fairly tame stuff at first, but she started to see the money come in, and saw what photos got the most likes and stuff, so she did more and went further."

"But why do that?" Kate asked.

"Because she wanted out. She hated living with her dad and wanted to move out. More money would allow her to do that."

"Makes sense," Jon commented. "And she was doing all this out of her bedroom, when she lived with her dad?"

Conrad nodded. "She'd do it when he wasn't around or busy doing something else. But, he found out eventually, and he hit the roof. He was furious with her and started to try and stop her from posting. She moved out as soon as she could when she was nineteen and stayed with friends until she started renting that house two years ago. Without her dad around anymore, she could do as much as she liked. I met her the following year."

"Did you know what she did for a living when you started dating?"

"Not right away, but she told me quite early on. There's no point in living a lie, after all. I'd find out eventually. It was a pretty big part of her life by then."

"And what did you think?"

"I supported her. She was making good money, and it was all fairly harmless, so, why not."

"You didn't mind that other people were seeing her naked?" Kate asked.

He shrugged. "No. If they weren't looking at her, they'd be looking at someone else, so why not her. Why not make money off them? It's just a human body, we've all got them and see them every day, and it's not as if they're in the room with her."

"No, I guess not," Jon replied, narrowing his eyes. "But she must attract some people who take more than a passing interest in her, right? She must have some quite dedicated fans. Obsessive fans even? Has she had any trouble with people finding out more than they should or getting a little too close?"

"Stalkers, you mean?"

Jon nodded.

"You think a stalker did this?" Conrad asked.

"I don't know. I'm just looking at this from all angles. So, did she have any?"

"Yeah," he said, seeming to think it through. "Yeah, there's been a few that seem a little more obsessive than the others. Two stand out, actually."

"Two?"

"Well, there's more. She gets weird messages all the time, but two of them have been a little more trouble than they're worth."

"Why?"

"Well... Okay, so the two I'm talking about are Ken and Ozzy. Ken... Well, he's just obsessive. He buys everything from her, from photos and things to used knickers, all that kind of stuff."

Jon noticed Kate pull a face out the corner of his eye at that last comment. "But, he kept his distance?"

"I think so. He's local, though. Doesn't live far away, and he somehow knew she was local too and has messaged a bunch of times, wanting to meet up with her. But she always turned him down."

"And, his name's Ken?" Kate asked.

"Yeah. Ken Wyndam. Goes by the name Wyndy on HoundPic."

"And the second one, Ozzy?"

"Ozzy... No, Ozzy is different. He's just as obsessive as Ken, but he's nasty with it. He started out all nicey nice, but over time, when she refused to do some of the things he asked, he turned nasty, and threatened to find her and kill her. He said some pretty disgusting stuff, actually. So we banned him. Not that it did much, because he joined up under a different username, and the same thing happened again."

"He turned nasty again?" Jon asked.

"Yep. Threatened to rape and kill her, all the usual."

"I see."

"We went through that cycle a few times, banning him and then working out he'd joined up again under a new username. It was a bit of a nightmare, actually. We'd started to talk to the support team on HoundPic about doing something a little more permanent, but we weren't far along that road."

"Another local?" Jon asked.

Conrad nodded. "It was another reason why he stood out from the other nut-jobs that message her."

"How do you know where they live?" Kate asked.

"They send their address when they want something sent over to them," Conrad said and shrugged. "Ozzy was blatant, and didn't seem to care."

"And you didn't mind her doing this, sending things to these guys?"

"Did you see the house she lived in?" Conrad asked, giving them a knowing look.

"Fair point," Kate remarked.

"I'm going to need as much information on these guys as possible," Jon said.

"Yeah, no problem. It's all in the messages in her profile, and I can dig out anything else you need."

"Thank you. Alright, was there anything else you can think of that might be useful? Any friends she'd fallen out with?

Was there anyone else you know who might want to hurt her?"

Conrad shook his head. "No, not really. She might have come from a rough family, but she was the sweetest girl you could ever hope to know. She wouldn't hurt a fly. Her friends all liked her."

"You're sure?" Kate asked.

"Okay, let me put it this way, I didn't know anyone else who didn't like her. But I guess that doesn't mean there wasn't."

"No, it does not," Jon admitted. It wasn't as if they needed more leads anyway. They had enough to keep them going for a while yet, just from this one interview.

6

"So, that's why they put you with me."

Nathan shrugged as he drove through the Surrey countryside in the early morning. The air was fresh, and a thick cloying mist lay low, veiled over the surrounding fields, with the occasional tree and hedgerow peeking up from the grey fog. The sun climbed from behind the hills, bathing the scene in a warm, golden glow, splashing colour across the scenery and making the cold air seem warmer than it had any right to be.

"Oh," Ellie said, looking over. "So, it's some kind of test of character for me to investigate a case with you?"

"It was, once upon a time, according to some," Nathan moderated, feeling ambivalent about the whole thing, as he thought back to his time on the Surrey Murder Team after his demotion. Those days were long gone though, and things were much better than they used to be. Working with Kate and then Jon had turned things around for him and put his career back on track. He was already climbing back up the ranks and hoped to regain his DCI rank one day.

"I'm sorry you had to go through that." Ellie's voice was full of feeling and empathy.

"It's fine, really. Don't worry about me."

"Okay." She shrugged. "From what you were talking about back in the office, it sounds like you've met this Elden Lichwood before?"

He drove on absentmindedly as he cast his mind back to the investigation into the Urbex Killer with Kate, and their visit to the Lichwood estate. Elden was a rich man. Wealthy, powerful and well connected. He was formidable, but apparently not invulnerable, it seemed.

"We have, Kate and I. It was back during the investigation of the Urbex Killer. The girls he murdered were all kidnapped at the same time from an abandoned mental asylum, and Elden owned it."

"The father of the killer owned the site where the victims were kidnapped from? How did he not know it was his son doing the kidnapping?"

Nathan shrugged. "Good question. In fact, I personally believe he did know. In fact, I think he actively helped Solomon, his son, plan the whole thing."

"Really?"

"I have no proof," he admitted. "There's nothing to support my theory, no evidence at all, but that's what I believe. He had to have noticed something odd going on with his son at the very least, but he says he knew nothing, and now he's taken his secret to the grave."

"So, you'll never know."

"Unless Solomon admits it, no."

"Or, unless we find something in Elden's house during this investigation."

"Yep. I could be vindicated yet," Nathan admitted as he approached the turn into the large Lichwood property. The house was out in the countryside, up on a hillside, looking out towards the Surrey Hills like a silent monolith, a sentinel in the wilderness, standing tall against the chill wind.

At the gates, Nathan spotted the familiar scene of the police line, guarded by uniformed officers who kept the already assembled press at bay while allowing official vehicles through.

Nathan turned in and pulled up towards the line and the waiting officer, pulling out his warrant card as he slowed.

"Detective Halliwell," a muffled voice shouted at him through the window. "Detective. What do you know about Mr Lichwood's death? Is it being treated suspiciously? Can you tell me anything?"

Nathan looked up and into the journalist's face and recognised the blogger and all-around annoying person, Scott Wells. After his little stunt with the last case, turning up at the kidnapper's location just as they went to arrest him, he was well known to the entire team.

Nathan's face must have displayed his recognition and dismay because Scott smiled at him and continued to shout at the car.

"Shit," Nathan hissed as he looked away and concentrated on easing the car into the property, through the electric gates, where he could finally leave the scrum behind.

"Problem?" Ellie asked.

"Hopefully not," Nathan replied. "I just recognised one of the bottom feeders back there. He was something of an annoyance on a recent case." That was an understatement if ever there was one. He could have got himself killed if not for Kate's quick thinking.

"Aaah, okay. Which one?"

"Scott Wells, he was at my window back there. He's a blogger, and he got a little too close to the last case. Nearly got himself murdered, the idiot."

"That's certainly is idiotic," Ellie confirmed. "I'll keep an eye out for him."

"Thanks," Nathan replied as they drove up towards the huge house that dwarfed the ranks of police vehicles parked out front. Usually, this much police presence on a scene created a cluttered and packed in feeling, but there was so much room on these grounds that Nathan wondered if they needed more people on site.

As they pulled up towards the front of the house, Nathan recalled his previous visit here and their encounter with Elden and his friend Grey. Grey had been leaving in his bright green Lamborghini as they'd pulled up.

A smile played across Nathan's lips as he remembered how Grey had attempted to sweet talk Kate with the promise of a ride in his car. Predictably, he'd not got very far. Kate was just too classy to fall for the rich man's simple ploy.

But the scene was very different to how things were back then, and the mood that filled the air was a sombre one.

"So, what do we know?" Ellie asked as they parked and got out of the car.

"Not much. Only that he was shot in his own home."

"Alright, let's go and have a look then."

Nathan smiled to himself, recognising some of Kate's keen drive in Ellie. He liked her already, he thought as they walked through the various cars and vans, getting directions towards the duty officer.

"Officers?" the uniformed sergeant in forensic overalls asked as they approached. The dark-haired woman wasn't tall, but she was stocky and powerful looking.

Nathan offered his hand. "DI Halliwell, and DC Mizaki."

"Sergeant Rosa Peaks." She gave Nathan's hand a firm shake. It felt like he was holding onto a rock rather than a hand. "It's a mess in there."

"Mr Elden Lichwood, right?"

"And a woman we haven't identified yet, yes. Suit up and we'll head inside."

They were soon dressed in their forensic coveralls and making their way into the building.

Rosa took the lead, glancing back as she spoke. "It looks like some kind of house invasion, but as far as we can tell, they didn't take anything. If I had to guess, they came here to kill, not to steal."

"With Elden being the target," Nathan stated.

"That would be my guess," Peaks agreed.

"Any CCTV or security footage?"

"There's cameras," Peaks confirmed. "We're looking into getting the footage."

They walked into the main front hallway of the house, where they found the first victim, a young woman in a silk robe who'd been shot. The deep red, dried blood on the marble floor framed her head, like some kind of sick halo as she gazed lifelessly towards the office on their left, where Nathan spotted further activity by forensics officers.

"This is how we found things," Peaks said. "We've not moved anything."

"Good." Crouching beside the dead woman, Nathan peered at the wound. It was small, located dead centre just between her eyes, and he could see the powder burn. It was an expert shot. "This looks like a professional job. She was executed at point-blank range. The gunman knew what he was doing."

"That was our assessment too," Peaks acknowledged.

"At least she didn't suffer," Ellie commented.

Nodding, Nathan considered that. It told them something about how this job went down, and what the killer was after. "No. That wasn't their objective. This was more like a job. The killer didn't want the victims to suffer, he just wanted them dead."

"Get in, do the deed, and get out," Ellie mused.

"Exactly." Nathan turned to the uniformed officer. "I'd like to see Elden, please."

"Certainly, this way."

"Who called this in?"

"When security was tripped, the firm that manages the estate was alerted, and so were we. Phone calls went unanswered, so we sent a car over to check it out. The gates were open and slightly damaged, which led to further investigation."

Nathan nodded as they walked into the study. "And the discovery of the bodies?"

"The front door was open," Peaks confirmed. "The officer who found the bodies called it in."

"Okay, thanks," Nathan replied as he walked into the opulent study. It was all dark woods, with rugs on the polished floor, vases with plants in them and shelves with books and photos arranged neatly.

The work lights of the forensic team, and their white-clad bodies, stood out in this wealthy environment. Peaks led them over to the second corpse. Elden was on his back, with a vacant, slightly shocked expression on his face, his eyes open, staring into the void. Like the girl, a single gunshot to the head was the only wound, and again, it was expertly placed.

"Killed quickly and cleanly," Nathan muttered. "Do we have any clues as to who did this?"

"There is one thing," Peaks said.

"Oh?" Nathan turned and looked back at Peak who'd remained standing beside him. She pointed back towards the door they'd entered through and some graffiti on the wall beside it.

Nathan got up and turned to face the design. It had been spray-painted in red and depicted a crude bat-winged creature with a tail and long neck.

"Any ideas what that might be?" Peaks asked.

"It's a dragon," Nathan stated, suddenly making a connection as he realised what had happened.

"A dragon?" Ellie asked. "Why would someone paint a dragon on the wall?"

"He's telling us who he is," Nathan replied as he thought back to the news that the team had got several months ago. As he thought back, deeper memories bubbled up from years ago, back when he was a respected detective, back when he was married and had been investigating a corrupt businessman who'd chosen to send Nathan a message.

"And who is he?" Ellie peered at the dragon.

"His nickname is The Dragon, but his real name is Terry Sims. He's a thug and a killer, and someone Kate and I put away around a year ago, only for him to recently escape prison. I was wondering where he'd turn up."

"You're sure?"

"Ninety-five percent sure," Nathan answered as images of Terry from his past flashed before his eyes. Grappling Terry in that garden, with Kate nearby as they took down him and Abban. Then further back, years ago, when Terry had stormed into his home, separated him from his now ex-wife, and beaten him to a pulp. "But the security footage should confirm it."

With the troubling memories foremost in his mind, he turned and walked away from the dragon logo. Nathan wandered over to a shelf decorated with several framed photos. He spotted the familiar faces of Elden and his son,

Solomon, smiling and gazing out from the pictures, showing them in happier times. Were they always cruel, heartless killers, or had something happened to them to make them this way?

"Tell me about this Terry," Ellie had followed him.

"Terry?" Nathan thought back. He pondered whether to tell Ellie more about his past and what had happened to him. He'd told Kate, but it wasn't something that was common knowledge. However, if Ellie was going to be working this case with him, she probably had a right to know. "He and I have something of a history, actually."

"Oh?"

"Yeah. It goes back to the case that got me promoted to DCI, before all that turned to shit."

"You were a DCI?"

"At one point, before I got demoted."

"I didn't know."

"No reason you should know. But yeah, I was working on a case, investigating a man called Sandford Barret who killed his mistress because she threatened to tell his wife and family about their affair. Sandford was dirty, though, and worked for Terry, who was a local thug who could get things done. If I remember rightly, Sandford was a business contact who laundered money for him. This was a while ago, though, so I might get a few details wrong."

"That's okay," Ellie replied.

"Anyway, I was getting quite close to having everything I needed to bring him in, and Sandford knew it, so he told Terry. One night, Terry stormed into my house, attacked us, and..."

That night was burned into his mind, and he could still feel the terror he'd gone through when Terry and his crew stormed into his house and dragged his wife away, screaming, before beating him up.

Things got a little murky then. He couldn't really remember much about what they did to him. He could pick out flashes of blood, violence, and crazy things that were probably his mind playing tricks on him. Until his wife woke him up and Terry was gone.

"I'm sorry, you don't need to tell me if you don't want to."

"It's fine. You should know. Terry beat me up, and I don't really remember much beyond that. But we both survived, and I continued with the case, putting Sandford away for a long time. I didn't see Terry for ages after that, until more recently, when I was investigating another house invasion. I was working with Kate. Terry was working for Abban Devlin, hunting for a book that he wanted. Terry was willing to kill to get it."

"A book?" Ellie asked, looking a little surprised.

"A very valuable book," Nathan explained.

"It had better be."

"Hmm. We tracked them down, and I ended up in a bit of a fight with Terry before I managed to arrest him."

"And now he's out again."

"That's right," Nathan confirmed. "Abban was a member of an organisation of rich, entitled men and women, who worked together for their own benefit and enrichment. They went by the name of the Black Hand and caused the deaths of several people in pursuit of their goals. They were ruthless, cruel people, but they've been somewhat quiet ever since we managed to arrest Abban. I always believed Elden was a member of this group, and I think this killing might prove it."

"Okay, so Terry worked for this organisation, and now he wants to kill them all?"

"He's pissed at them. During his trial, he testified that he was the mastermind behind everything that had happened. He tried to take the blame for it all, no doubt on the orders of the organisation. He was trying to keep Abban out of jail, but it didn't work, and Abban ended up locked up anyway. I like to think that the work Kate and I did in assembling the evidence before handing it over to the legal team played a hand in that."

"So Terry took the fall for his boss, only for his boss to end up in jail as well anyway, and now he's pissed about it."

"That's my guess. I'd be upset too if I ended up with a harsher sentence for no reason."

"Yeah, makes sense," Ellie agreed. "Now he's broken out of prison and taking his anger out on those who ruined his life."

"That's about the size of it."

"Alright. Do we know who else is a member of this group?"

"No. Not really. Abban was the only one we knew for certain. I suspected Elden was but didn't know for sure."

"Until now," Ellie finished for him.

"Yep, until now. So we know who did it, but we don't know who he'll hit next or where he is," Nathan surmised.

"Perfect," Ellie grunted.

7

Jon pulled up to the side of the road. He craned his neck to look out the windscreen and peer at the house one door along. He screwed his mouth up as he noticed the differences between it and its neighbours.

As semi-detached former council houses went, it was actually very well maintained and in a better shape than the dwellings that surrounded it. The front face was clean and recently painted, and the garden was in good condition. It wasn't what Jon had been expecting, he had to admit, but this job was full of surprises.

"Alright, thanks. Keep me informed." Kate ended the call and slumped in her seat, letting her hand, and the phone it held, drop to her lap. She seemed disappointed.

"No luck?" Jon asked her.

"Nope. No one's in at his home address." She gave him a look. "They have several other addresses that he's known to frequent, so they'll keep looking."

Jon gave a short nod by way of reply, feeling the same frustration that Kate was no doubt experiencing.

After some discussion following the interview with Conrad, they'd chosen to focus on the family first, while Dion and the others hunted down the HoundPic fans. They already had her dad and brother's addresses, and Jon felt like they were possibly the two people most invested in Jess's life. Her choice of career almost certainly had the most impact on them, too.

Besides, murder victims were usually killed by people who knew them, and knew them well.

Once that had been decided, Jon sent a team to bring in Jess's brother, Henry, while he and Kate opted to visit her father Mickey, and interview him at his home, the same home that Jess had once lived in. He was curious to see the environment Jess had been brought up in and speak to Mickey on home territory. Maybe it would tell them something about her family life that might shed some light on the case?

"Well, I hope they find him," Jon mused, as he looked back at Mickey's house. He nodded at it. "He keeps it in good nick."

"He's a labourer, isn't he? Works on building sites and such like?"

"Yeah. I guess it makes sense that his home looks good." Jon wondered if that played into all this too. Was he someone who cared about his stature in the local community and what others thought? If he was, then having a daughter exposing herself online might tarnish that.

"Did Jess's career choice cast a shadow over their family?" Kate mused, voicing Jon's thoughts.

"Exactly what I was thinking."

"Great minds and all that," Kate said.

"Either that or I'm dragging you down to my level."

"No chance. It's quite the opposite, I'm sure."

"Probably," Jon relented. "You're no doubt yanking me up by the lug-holes."

"The what-holes?"

"Lug-holes," Jon repeated. "Ears, Kate. By my ears."

"How charming."

"It worked on you, duck."

"I see your northern side is fighting back." Kate giggled.

"I let the beast out, every once in a while."

Kate snorted. "Yeah, right, you big softy. Come on, we need to get in there and see what's up with Jess's dad. He's certainly a suspect as far as I'm concerned."

"Me too. The disappearance of Jess's mum is suspect as all hell."

"And some," Kate agreed. "If he killed his wife, it's probably not a stretch for him to kill his daughter, too."

"That's a gruesome thought," he admitted. Any man capable of killing his wife was a man who was capable of anything. Killing Jess would be the least of his worries, especially if he hated Jess as much as Conrad seemed to think he did.

"He knows about his daughter's death, right?" Kate asked.

"Officers have already been round," Jon confirmed. "They know we're coming."

They climbed out of the car. Jon gazed up and down Leatherhead Street.

"You don't live far from here." Jon looked over at Kate.

"No, just around the corner," Kate mused. She glanced over at Jon. "If there are killers this close to me, maybe I should look at moving?"

Jon raised his eyebrows, thinking about Kate's earlier comment about moving in. "Oh, is that right?"

She shrugged.

"Are you suggesting something?" Jon asked, cocking his head to one side.

"I'm quite sure I have no idea what you're talking about," Kate said and then gave him a cheeky wink.

"Yeah, right."

They turned into the driveway and walked towards the house, which was set several metres back from the road, with a modest garden behind its white fence. Mickey had done a respectable job, and it was certainly one of the better-looking properties.

As they approached, the front door opened, making Jon briefly slow and tense as he wondered if Mickey was attempting to make a run for it. But instead, it was DC Faith Evanson, their unit's victim support officer. She waited for them to approach, and waved them forward in greeting. "Sir. Kate."

"Evanson," Jon greeted her. She must have been here waiting for them. "Everything okay?"

"Fine," she said and leant closer as she lowered her voice. "He's not said much but doesn't seem very upset."

"No?"

Faith gave her head a quick shake.

"Okay, let's have a chat," Jon suggested.

"Sir," Faith said and led them inside, where he found Mickey slumped on his sofa, staring at his phone. He scrolled with his thumb, so was probably on social media rather than doing anything vital.

"Mr Thornton?" Jon asked as he walked into the room.

Mickey closed his eyes for a moment and took a long breath before looking up and placing his phone on the arm of the chair, face down. Mickey tipped his head up and met Jon's eyes. "Yeah?"

"I'm Detective Pilgrim, and this is Detective O'Connell. I'm sorry for your loss, Mr Thornton. I understand this must be a difficult time for you, but we'd like to ask you some questions if that's okay?"

"Sure, why not. It's not as if I haven't answered hundreds of them already." He sighed. "Let's get this over with."

He seemed more annoyed and frustrated with their presence, than upset over the loss of his daughter from the way he was acting. Jon had visited plenty of parents who'd lost children in violent attacks, and most were either shocked or upset. Occasionally he came across someone who didn't quite know how to deal with the news and acted strangely, but he wasn't sure he'd seen ambivalence before.

Doing his best to keep his surprise and suspicion to himself, he sat down. "Okay, thank you. Just so you know, if you need to take a mome—"

"Just get on with it," Mickey replied.

"...uh, yeah, sure. Of course. As I'm sure you're aware, Mr Thornton, your daughter was found in the early hours of today, and it appears she was murdered. Do you know anyone who you think might want to do that to her?"

"Not really, no. One of her stalkers, maybe?"

"A stalker?"

"That's what I said."

"Were you aware of any stalkers?"

"No. But she's bound to have some."

"And why's that?" Jon decided to push him on this, and see what Mickey thought of Jess's profession. Would it match up to what Conrad said?

"Because of what she did." Sure enough, he was already sounding annoyed.

"You mean, the photos she took of herself?"

Mickey chewed on his lip. "Yeah, that's right. Those things."

"So, you were aware of the way she made money."

"Yeah." Mickey glanced up, before looking away again.

"And what did you think about it?"

Mickey stiffened and met Jon's eyes again. "What does that have to do with anything?" There was a note of suspicion in his voice. Jon wanted to dig deeper here, but they'd barely started, and he didn't want Mickey cutting the interview short before they'd got going.

"We're just trying to build up a picture of her life and relationships, Mr Thornton, so please don't read anything into the questions we might ask you. We're not suggesting anything."

"Good."

"So, did you approve of Jess's profession?" Kate asked, jumping in.

Mickey glanced at Kate and then back at Jon, his eyes narrowed in uncertainty. "No, it's disgusting. I didn't like to think of her like that."

"I'm sure no father would." Jon tried to sound reassuring. "Putting herself out there, like that, it has to be a little risky."

"Yeah, I guess."

"So you don't know of any stalkers?"

"Not any in particular," Mickey admitted. "I told you, I don't take much interest in what she does. She doesn't live with me anymore, so what she does with her life is none of my business, is it? Stupid girl. She should have seen this coming. I told her, I did. I told her no good would come of this. And that bloody boyfriend of hers too. Have you been looking into him? He's a piece of work. Why would he support her… you know…" He waved his hands before his chest, as if pulling out some imaginary boobs.

Jon cut in. "…in doing something that she loved?"

Mickey locked eyes with him. "He's just as perverted as she was. That's all I know." He looked away. "Hmm, something she loved? She didn't love it. How could she love it?"

"How do you know she hated it?" Kate asked.

"Because how could anyone love doing that? She's been showing the world her… her bits… You know? That's not right? There must have been something wrong in her head for her to want to do that. It's messed up. I blame her mother, you know? That's where she gets it from. She didn't get it from me, that's for sure."

"Cathy Thornton," Kate stated.

"Your missing wife," Jon added.

"Yeah. That bitch. She was as bad as Jessica was until she just disappeared on me, leaving Jess and me and her son."

"Henry," Kate clarified, putting a name to Jess's brother.

"Why didn't you like Jess doing this?" Jon asked. "Did you feel embarrassed? Did it upset you?"

"You're damn right it did," he snapped. "No dad wants their child to do something like that. I gave her a home, food, I looked after her, and this is how she repays me? She was spitting in my face."

"Those are some strong words," Kate suggested.

Mickey shrugged. "So what? I didn't agree with what she was doing, and I'm entitled to my opinion."

"What did Henry think of what she did?" Jon asked.

"He hated it too," Mickey replied.

"As much as you do, or more?"

"I don't know."

"Tell me about Cathy," Kate asked, cutting in. "She left you, didn't she?"

"Yeah, she did. Out of the blue, it was. She disappeared one night while I was asleep. I just woke up, and she was gone. She left all of us behind. She didn't care about any of us."

"And why would she do that, Mr Thornton?" Kate pressed. "Why would she just leave? There has to be a reason."

"I don't know," he replied with a shrug, his eyes roaming the room.

"You have no idea?"

"No."

"And you don't know where she might be now?"

Kate was pushing him on this, and Mickey seemed to squirm a little under her questions.

"No. Why would I?" Mickey asked. "I don't know why she left me or where she went, just like I don't know who killed Jess or why. Alright? But I suggest you start asking some of the sick fucks who were looking at those photos she posted online and stop bothering me…"

Mickey stopped and looked away, his eyes staring into the middle distance for a moment before they snapped back to Jon and Kate. "You think I killed her, don't you?"

"We never said that, Mr Thornton," Jon said.

"You don't need to. I know what you're doing. This is a shakedown, isn't it? You want to see how I react to things and see if I slip up or do something ridiculous. Well, screw you. I didn't kill her, alright. Do you understand? Do I make myself clear?"

"Please, calm down..."

"Hell no. I won't bloody well calm down, you fucking pigs. You're all the same, coming round the council estates, bothering us when we've done nothing wrong. It's discrimination it is. That's what it is." He got to his feet and was shouting at them, waving his arms around. "This interview is over. Go on, get out. Get out of here."

There was little they could do without further evidence, so they left with Mickey shouting after them before he slammed the door behind them. Faith Evanson, the victim support officer, was with them too, having not escaped Mickey's wrath.

"That went about as well as I thought it might," Faith said as they walked up the driveway, away from the house. Jon glanced back and could see a shadowy figure in the front room, watching them as they walked off his property.

"Was he as friendly as that with you?"

"He didn't shout at me if that's what you're asking. But then, I wasn't asking the difficult questions, so..."

"Fair point," Jon agreed. "So, what was your impression of the man?"

"I think there's reason enough to suspect him of something. Those were not the reactions of a normal parent who's lost their child," Faith replied.

"I agree," Kate said. "I think we'll be talking to him again soon."

8

Nathan navigated his way through the form on his screen, entering details of what they had discovered in the Lichwood mansion in text box after text box. Gone were the days of the typewriter and handwritten records. Instead, they were replaced with flat screens and online systems.

He wasn't sure which he preferred. The computer was great, no doubt, with its access to a vast database that linked everything up and made connecting seemingly separate cases so much easier. And yet, he sometimes missed the days of paper and ink. There was something satisfying and real about holding a file in his hand, bulging with evidence, reports, and facts about the crimes he was investigating.

Would he go back?

Probably not. But he was a long way off from touch typing or being as fast as some of the younger officers on the machines that sat on every desk in this room.

Glancing over at Ellie as her hands flew over the keyboard, her fingers hitting keys without her even looking, he was envious of her skill with the tools they had at their disposal.

It was early days, and yet, these few hours he'd spent with Ellie had already impressed him. She was calm, thoughtful, and focused on the job. There was potential in her, that was for certain, and he could see her rising through the ranks with little trouble. The gruesome scenes at the crime scene hadn't fazed her either, which was always a good thing.

He remembered the first scene he'd visited with Kate after she'd joined the Murder Team, and her reaction to seeing that first body strung up in the tree. She'd taken a moment, and he'd assumed the dead body had turned her stomach. Her reaction had made him wonder if she'd be cut out for the job. But he needn't have worried.

Without all the facts, he'd made an assumption and an incorrect one at that. Kate was not at all bothered by the sight of a dead body. Instead, it had been the circumstances they had found the body in that had struck a nerve with her. The ritual nature of the crime and the occult influence, it had all reminded her of how her aunt had been killed. It was the memories of that moment that had upset her.

That was all dealt with now, as much as it could be, and Kate had proven herself to be a capable detective during her first case and continued to impress ever since.

He had little doubt that Ellie would follow a similar path of success and dedication to the job.

Nathan's desk phone rang, making him jump. He picked it up. "Yep?"

"It's Jon. Have you got a moment?"

Nathan turned and glanced across the room. He saw Jon at his office desk. He waved.

"Be right there."

"Bring Ellie," Jon said and ended the call.

Nathan got up. "Right then, young one, we've got a meeting with the boss. Jon wants to see us."

"Oh, okay. What's up?"

"No idea. He might want an update. Let's go and see what's cooking, hey?"

Ellie left her desk and followed him across the room and into Jon's office, where Nathan found the DCI sitting behind his desk. Kate and one of their civilian investigators were also in the room.

"Come in, Nathan, Ellie. How's things going?"

"Alright," Nathan replied. "We were just doing some of the paperwork."

"Was it Elden?" Kate asked.

"Yep," Nathan said, his tone serious. "Him and a woman we don't know. Both were executed with a single shot to the head."

"Executed?" Jon asked. "You're sure?"

"Pretty sure, and I think I know who did it."

"Already?"

"We found a dragon spray-painted onto the wall, and I'm willing to bet the CCTV will confirm that it was Terry Sims."

"Who refers to himself as The Dragon," Kate added under her breath, finishing the thought.

"Exactly," Nathan confirmed.

"Shit, so he's taking revenge," Kate mused.

"That would be my assumption," Nathan admitted. "He's going after the people who he used to work for. The people who screwed him over."

"That's great work," Jon said. "And fits with some new information we've just had come in." He turned and looked over at the other woman standing in the room. "Ellie, this is Debbie Constable, one of our civilian investigators. Debbie?"

Debbie gave Jon a curt nod and turned to Nathan and Ellie. "Hi. I was telling Jon that we've just had a call from High Down Prison about Abban, and how Terry Sims managed to get to him."

"I take it they were separated from one another, then?" Nathan asked, reading between the lines.

"Correct, they were," Debbie confirmed. "In fact, Terry didn't even know Abban was in the same prison for a while. But unfortunately for Abban, they had a mutual friend. A prisoner called Lester Harris, who, for reasons unknown at this point, managed to somehow bring Terry and Abban together. Terry attacked Abban and not long after managed to escape the prison entirely."

"I can't say I feel sorry for Abban," Nathan muttered.

"Me neither," Kate said.

"He's not in a good way," Debbie said. "They're unsure if he'll survive, and if he does, there might be some permanent damage."

"The world will be better without him," Kate added.

"You'll get no argument from me about that," Nathan said. "Who's this, Lester Harris?"

"A violent criminal," Debbie said. "His record says he's been done for assault as well as some online crime. Hacking and stuff."

"And can we get to see him?" Nathan asked. "We can head over to High Down now."

"Actually, he's already out. He got out a short while after Terry escaped. He served his sentence and was released," Debbie explained. "I have his details and his address."

"Excellent, thank you, Debbie," Nathan replied and turned to Ellie. "I think we should have a word with Lester."

She nodded. "Absolutely."

"Kate, do you want in on this?" Jon asked, looking over at her.

Kate shook her head. "No, thanks." She looked up at Nathan. "You can handle this. I'm done with Abban and his shit."

Nathan gave her a single nod, fully understanding where Kate was coming from. He wasn't terribly keen on jumping back into the Abban, Terry, Black Hand thing again either, but he was undoubtedly the best man for the job given his history and familiarity with the details.

He couldn't help feeling like he was wading back into the shit again, though, after having just cleaned it all off from the first time he'd dealt with these goons. But Terry was out there, and he had unfinished business with that man. He needed to find him, bring him in, and hopefully lock him up for a long time. He'd be placed in the highest security prison in the land after this little stunt, and for Nathan's money, they could lock him up and throw away the key. The world was a better place without him.

"Is that alright?" Jon asked.

"Of course, guv. We'll get this done." He turned to Ellie again. "Won't we?"

"We will," she confirmed with a nod and a smile before she narrowed her eyes. "One thing, though, if you don't mind me asking..."

"Go on," Jon encouraged her.

"What's the deal with this man, Abban? Were you the one to arrest him, Kate?"

Kate raised her eyebrows and seemed to take a moment as she arranged her thoughts.

Jon guessed that was not an easy task where Abban was concerned, though.

Ellie glanced at him as Kate took a moment.

"I... I didn't mean to pry," Ellie added. She was probably worried that she'd upset Kate.

"No, don't worry, it's fine," Kate said, raising her hand in a calming gesture. "Abban Devlin and I have something of a history. Back when I was a teenager, he killed my Aunt in Ireland and then proceeded to taunt me via handwritten letters for the next ten years or something."

"Really? Holy shit. I'm sorry..."

"Don't be. It's all over now that he's in jail. But I don't really feel like taking on any case involving him again."

"Of course, I understand," Ellie said. "I'm sorry."

Kate gave her a slight smile while again rubbing her finger.

"Do you have any leads on Terry?" Jon asked, moving them away from the subject of Abban.

"No, none, actually. I have a file on him which I'll go through. We know his haunts from before prison and the people he hung out with. But Terry isn't an idiot, and will realise we know about them too. So I doubt that will throw anything up."

"You never know." Jon shrugged.

"True," Nathan agreed.

"What about targets?" Jon asked.

"That's a tough one," Nathan replied. "He'll be going after the remaining members of the organisation he used to work for, but we don't have a confirmed list of members or anything close to one."

This was despite his best efforts to assemble such a list back in the days of the killing spree they went on, when he and Kate were on the Murder Team.

"How about Grey Davison?" Kate suggested.

Nathan raised his eyebrows and nodded. "Yeah, maybe. We only met him once, though, at Elden's, and that doesn't mean he was a part of the same organisation."

"No," Kate agreed. "But he is a millionaire playboy, and he and Elden did seem friendly. He fits the type."

"True," Nathan agreed. "I bet you're glad you didn't get into his Lamborghini."

Kate gave him a wry smile. "Despite what you might think, fast cars really aren't a way to a girl's heart."

"That's why I drive a Volvo."

Kate snorted. "Touché."

"Take a look at Grey," Jon suggested.

"I will," Nathan agreed. "I'll pull out my previous research into the group, see if that throws up anything useful. I'll get Lester in too."

"Sounds good."

9

"The Dragon, Hmm?" Jon said to Kate once Nathan, Ellie and Debbie had left the room.

She sighed and hung her head for a moment. "Yeah, looks like it."

"He was that bald thug you told me about, the one who helped Abban, right?" He'd discussed the Abban case with her several times during his time down here, mainly after that first case, and was aware that she'd tangled with him before.

"That's the one." She didn't look up.

"Are you worried?" Jon studied her as she played with her injured finger in her lap. He tried to read her mood and wondered how much was getting to her.

She let out another long breath. "No, not really."

"Are you sure?"

She looked up. "Honestly, no. I'm fine. I'm concerned about him being out there and potentially hurting more people, but I'm not worried about myself. Also, Nathan's a capable detective, and Ellie looks like she's on the job, so..."

"They can handle it," Jon finished.

"Yeah, they can." She went quiet and contemplative again. Jon wasn't sure what to say next and allowed the moment to spread its wings. It wasn't an uncomfortable silence. They were way past that now in their relationship and were quite happy just being in each other's company and not talking if neither of them felt like it.

Glancing up at Kate again, he wondered if she was just trying to reassure him by saying she wasn't worried. Maybe she was concerned about him taking her off duty for a while or doing the opposite and assigning her to the case. He wouldn't do either, of course. He wanted Kate where he could watch out for her, and where she was happiest.

"Back on that Abban case," Kate said suddenly, without facing him as if she was thinking out loud. "Towards the end, we found out where Terry was based and stormed the building where they were holed up with a firearms unit. We had some kind of NCA affiliated agent with us that Damon brought with him. She was like a badass female James Bond, or something. We went in there and took out Terry's crew, and I ended up shooting two of them."

"You used a gun?"

Kate nodded, and glanced up briefly. "Yeah. I've had firearms training. You?"

"No." He'd never seen the need for him to do it. But hearing that Kate had trained and used a gun in the line of duty was surprising. He found it difficult to imagine. "Did you kill them?"

"Nope. I put a bullet in the gut of a man called Doug Turner, and shot a woman called Mel Garner in the leg. Both survived and were arrested."

"Wow," Jon muttered. "And you remember their names?"

"It's kind of difficult to forget something like that, besides, I've kept half an eye on them since."

"And...? What happened to them?"

"Both got off, pretty much scot-free," Kate said. "Mel got a token sentence that she served easily before she was let out early, and Doug never even saw any jail time."

Jon pulled a face. "The system doesn't always work."

"No, it doesn't, and those two people are out there."

"Do you think they'll come after you?" It was an obvious conclusion to come to. Otherwise, why tell him? Was she warning him, letting him know that there were people out there who wanted her dead?

Kate shrugged. "I honestly don't know. I would doubt it. They seemed like professionals to me, and they've not come after me yet."

"Do you think they joined up with Terry?"

"I don't know. All I do know is that we lost track of them around the time that Terry escaped. We have no idea where they are."

"Shit." The information troubled him. "Does Nathan know?"

"Yeah. We've been quietly keeping tabs on them."

"Good. Nathan knows what he's doing." Sitting back, he glanced over at his monitor and the details of their current case. He'd been analysing the information they had on Mickey Thornton following their disaster of an interview.

"Mickey really didn't help his case today, did he," Jon said as he let his eyes rove across the screen.

Kate smirked. "No, not really. He was acting terribly sus."

"Sus?"

"Oh yeah, I'm down with the kids Jon, didn't you know? I'm up on all the latest slang, brah."

Jon cracked a smile. "You're so not cool."

"Nah fam, I'm hip and happnin' y'all."

He tried to hold back, but the awkward made-up gang signs she was throwing up with her hands, looked more like some kind of flailing squid than a scary gang-banger. He laughed, and after a moment, Kate joined him.

Composing himself, Jon brought the conversation back to the topic at hand. "So, what do we do about Mickey? Do we leave him or have another chat? I think there's something there."

"No, I think we just need to watch him. How about we pop some surveillance on him for a few days. Just get someone to watch him and follow him around a bit? If he has done something, we might have just spooked him enough that he'll do something stupid."

The idea was sound. "Alright, sounds good. I'm happy with that. I'll make some calls and get that authorised. I'll tell them to report to you, okay?"

"Perfect," Kate said with a smile.

On his desk, his PC pinged, and a message popped up from DS Rachel Arthur. The pathologist had concluded her examination of the body.

"What's up?" Kate asked.

"Fancy a trip somewhere cold and sterile, filled with dead bodies?"

"Oh my, how could I resist that?" Kate answered. "You had me at dead bodies."

"I know all the best lines."

"Shame they only work on your work colleagues, hey?"

***

Jon held the door for Kate as he walked into the main examination room at the mortuary. They were greeted by a smell best described as a mix of death and cleaning products. He wasn't sure he could ever get used to it, and yet, there was Aileen at a nearby desk, taking a bite from a granola bar as she tapped keys on a PC. She smiled and wiped away a random crumb from her lip as they entered.

"Aaah, there you are," Aileen said and stuffed the wrapper back into her lunch box. "Glad you could join us."

Jon glanced sideways, wondering who else she was talking about and concluded that she was most likely referring to the dead bodies.

"Any time," Jon replied, giving her a smile. "I sent Rachel back to the station." He jabbed his thumb towards the door, referring to the brief conversation he'd had with the DS outside. She'd been present for the examination to make notes and answer questions. But the job was done now.

"No problem." Aileen moved to a nearby sink and started washing her hands.

"She said you'd finished your examination of Jess."

"I have indeed. If you bear with me for a moment, I'll just get cleaned up, and we'll have a chat. She's over there, by the way."

Jon followed her nod, spotted the table with a covered body on it, and grimaced at the knowledge that he'd be seeing what was beneath that sheet in short order. Turning to Kate, she didn't look too impressed with the idea either.

Moments later, wearing protective clothing, Aileen joined them and led them over to the table, where she pulled back the sheet to reveal Jess's pale, cold and impassive face. Her eyes were closed, and the cuts on her face had been sewn shut. She seemed peaceful, not at all as he'd remembered her back in the room they'd first seen her in. The damage to her face was severe though, and it looked like she'd been slashed across the face several times, cutting through her skin, lips and even an eyelid.

Aileen started to go through her notes and list the injuries that Jess had received during the attack, pulling the sheet back as she showed them more of the horror that had been inflicted upon Jess. Like her face, the wounds had been treated and closed, her skin puckered and pulled together by the stitches, with patches of red and purple scattered over her otherwise pale skin.

The list of injuries was long and tragic. Jon couldn't help but stare at Jess's face as Aileen spoke and wonder how much she'd suffered.

The thought of it mixed with the horror show before him was nearly enough to make him sick. It was only his previous experience and seeing other victims that saved him from losing his lunch.

"All in all, she's suffered about as much as anyone I've ever had come through here," Aileen commented. "Also, judging from the injuries and the order in which the attacker inflicted them, she was likely alive for much of it."

"She went through hell," Jon muttered.

"She did."

He turned to look at Kate. "So what does this tell us?"

"Well," Kate said, "he cut up her breasts, and her groin, stabbing her repeatedly."

"Correct," Aileen said. "He focused on her sexual organs as if he wanted to destroy what made her female."

"So, this guy hates women?" Jon guessed.

"I would assume so," Aileen replied. "He didn't rape Jess, but his crime was no less sexually motivated."

"This wasn't just an attack on Jess," Kate said. "This wasn't just personal to her. This was an attack on all women. You know what? I think he's an Incel."

"A what?" Jon asked.

"Incel," Kate replied. "Involuntarily Celibate. Men who desire sex but find themselves unable to get any, and so hate women for the rejection."

"Well, they sound like lovely people," Jon quipped. "And you think that Jess was killed by one?"

"An extreme one, maybe," Kate said.

"That fits," Aileen replied. "While I was working on her, I was reminded of Jack the Ripper and the way he would mutilate his victims. It's not exactly the same, but it's certainly similar."

"I think we can rule out the possibility of it being Jack himself," Jon said.

"He could be a fan of Jack's," Kate replied. "Someone who thinks of himself in the same way. Maybe he wants that same kind of infamy?"

"Either that, or this really is a jilted fan," Jon countered and shrugged. "If they'd become obsessed with Jess and with the idea of being with her, rejection might upset them enough that they end up doing this. The attack on her sexuality could be a form of revenge. He was destroying what she was using to make money."

"That works," Kate said, as she wandered around the table in thought. "The same reasoning could be used by her dad or brother if it was them. They know what she does for a living, and if she'd pushed them far enough, this could be how they take revenge on her. They hate what she does and attack her, focusing on her femaleness and what she was using to lure in the fans."

"That's a lot of options," Jon said. "So either we're looking at a random Incel, a Ripper fan-boy, a jilted fan, or a furious family member taking revenge. Either way, I think what she did as her job played a part. This attack on her sexuality feels like too much of a coincidence, given she was basically selling softcore porn and doing well out of it. That's certainly something that could have the potential to piss off a lot of jealous men."

"I agree," Kate confirmed. "This all comes back to her online persona."

Jon stood over the body for a moment, considering the options they had thrown into the ether, and the growing list of suspects. They had a lot of work to do.

"All done?" Aileen asked.

"For now," Jon answered. "Thank you, Doctor."

"Any time." She threw the sheet back over the body, hiding her from view once more.

10

Scott stood in the lobby of the high rise and sucked in a deep breath.

In front of him, the receptionist, a man in a prim suit, held the phone to his ear as he tapped in a number.

Finished, he looked up and raised an eyebrow on meeting Scott's gaze, as if his very presence offended him.

Scott smiled but felt awkward and turned, taking a couple of steps away from the desk as he gazed out through the glass doors at Croydon Street. Cars rolled by in the afternoon light, while people went about their work or shopping, or whatever they were doing in the centre of town.

He screwed his face up at the scene.

A Guildford boy at heart, he hated coming here. Croydon was about as close as Surrey came to a city, with its tall buildings around the main high street. He was aware that the city centre had doubled for Gotham in one of the Batman films at some point, which he supposed was a compliment.

But Croydon had a reputation as a rough area, and he always felt nervous coming here. He'd need to get used to the feeling if he was going to be any kind of half-decent journalist, though. You didn't get to pick and choose where the news happened. Besides, he'd surprised himself a few weeks back when he'd followed Detective Pilgrim and found him confronting that child kidnapper on the bridge.

Thinking about it now, it felt like it had been someone else because what he'd done sounded insane. And yet, he'd done it, and he'd survived.

He put some of that confidence down to Ariadne and the belief she had in him and his work. She'd taken him on and given him the chance to really make a go of it. As long as he reported back to her, she'd fund him and his work, making sure he always had what he needed. It was a wonderful feeling to be able to focus on his career full time and one day turn his blog into a reputable news source.

He still had a long way to go on that front, but he was already making great progress, and it was all because of her and her support.

"Mr Wells?"

Scott turned to the receptionist, who sneered down his nose at him as if he was some kind of unwanted stain on the floor. "Yes?"

"She says to go up. She's in the penthouse. Do you know where you're going?"

He nodded. "I'm sure I can figure it out."

The man raised a disapproving eyebrow and held it for a good second before replying. "Very well."

Leaving the stuck-up door-man to his self-important tasks, Scott strode over to the bank of lifts and called one down with a press of the button. Moments later, the brushed aluminium doors glided open with a whisper and granted him entry into its polished confines. Everything about this building screamed wealth at the top of its lungs. There wasn't a speck of dust on anything. All the surfaces were clean, free of greasy handprints, and sparkling. The inside of the lift was no different, with its mirrored walls and gold housing, lit with lights set carefully in the ceiling, and yet hidden from view by the clever design of this box that ferried people up and down the building.

There was only one button marked as 'penthouse', and it was all on its own at the top of the panel. Reaching out, he pressed it, but the button didn't change. Noticing a small glowing red LED beside it, he felt suddenly watched and glanced at the reception desk. The man behind it fake smiled and tapped the screen of his PC.

The red light turned green.

Realising the button had been locked, Scott pulled a face at the receptionist's petty behaviour, and pressed it again. Sure enough, the doors closed, just as smoothly and quietly as they'd opened, before the lift began to move.

"Prick," he muttered under his breath.

Catching sight of himself in the mirror, Scott smoothed his shirt and pulled a face at the creases that covered it. He didn't look his best, he had to admit, which was probably why the receptionist treated him like some kind of homeless person who'd wandered in off the street, begging for money or food.

Well, there was nothing for it now, he was already here, and there was no time for him to find a change of clothes.

He just hoped she wouldn't mind.

The lift slowed, and a moment later, with the most expensive-sounding ping he'd ever heard, the doors slid open, revealing a small lobby. Scott stepped out and noted there were only two doors in the small room other than the lift. One was clearly marked as the stairs, but the other was a clean white door with gold inlay, adorned with a single word. Penthouse.

That must be it, he thought and crossed the lobby, noting how soft and full the carpet felt beneath his feet. It was almost an abomination to walk on it with the shoes he'd worn on the street.

Reaching the door, he found it very slightly ajar, and for a moment, he hesitated.

"Come in, Mr Wells," called out a silky female voice from inside the room. Recognising the voice right away, he pushed the door open with renewed confidence and stepped into a spacious hallway.

"Make sure to close it behind you," the woman said from somewhere out of sight. Scott did as she asked, and the door made a satisfying click as it closed.

The hall was light and airy, with pearl coloured marble flooring and pale walls, decorated with modern abstract art canvases that were little more than splashes of colour. He had little doubt they would be expensive, but he wasn't a fan of the style.

He felt distinctly out of place in this minimalist, modern home, like a smear of dog shit on the polished marble. But he needed to tell her about the case he was investigating, and when she'd invited him here, he couldn't really refuse.

Besides, he'd been curious to see where she lived.

Scott crept deeper into the apartment, craning his neck as he looked left and right into more huge rooms with expensive furniture.

How the other half lived!

"I'm through here, Mr Wells, don't keep me waiting," she called out. Scott snapped upright and followed the voice to his right, moving out of the entrance hall and around to a side room where he found the woman sitting behind a desk, her legs crossed as she lounged back, looking at him from beneath hooded eyes.

"Don't look so scared, Mr Wells. I won't bite."

"Ariadne. Thank you for seeing me."

"But of course. I'm always happy to see the people I invest in." She frowned. "Are you short of money? You look a little scruffy."

Scott stiffened at the comment and smoothed his shirt again. "Um, no, I'm okay."

"Nonsense, I'll pop some funds over to you. I want you to sort your wardrobe out. I suggest throwing everything in it away and starting over, based on... that. I can't have you looking like a scruff if you're working for me, Mr Wells. Is ten thousand okay?"

"Wuh... what? Ten... Ten thousand? You mean pounds?"

She grimaced. "Hmm, no, you're right, that's not quite enough, is it. I'll make it fifteen."

Scott could only blink at her offer. He was utterly stunned. She'd already paid him handsomely for the work so far, but this was just for clothes. His mind boggled at the idea that she could be so blasé with that amount of money.

"Thank you."

"Pleasure. Now, Mr Wells, why did you visit and make my place look dirty?"

"Um, well. I thought you'd like to know about a case that I've been looking into, that the SIU are taking on."

"The SIU? You were right to come to me, I'm always interested in what DCI Pilgrim is up to. Please, go on." She chewed on the end of a pen and settled into her chair. He could see the red sole of the stiletto heeled shoe she wore on her raised foot. "Thrill me with your journalism, Mr Wells."

"Do you know who Elden Lichwood is?"

Ariadne narrowed her eyes. "Hmm, yes. I've heard the name before. A rich businessman, isn't he?"

"My sources inform me he was found dead earlier today. I was tipped off through one of my contacts and got to the scene with a few other members of the press, only for us to be dispersed a short time later."

"Hmm, I've not heard of this. This should be big news."

"I know. But Lichwood's lawyers have stopped the news being reported, at least for the time being. I'm sure it will get out, but right now, I can't report it without opening myself up to legal action."

"I see. What else do you know?"

"Not much. I can't even confirm that Elden is dead yet. All I have is hearsay from my contacts."

"Well, let's see if I can't rectify that," she said and picked up her phone. Scott watched as she focused on it, tapping away on the screen with her thumbs for a few seconds before she placed the phone back on the desk and looked up. "What do you know about Mr Lichwood?"

"Not much," Scott confirmed. "He was something of a recluse. He's a billionaire, I know that, and a well connected one with friends in all the right places. There have been some allegations against him over the years, but nothing stuck. There's also the matter of his son, Solomon, who killed several young women a year or so back. Detective Kate O'Connell and Nathan Halliwell led that investigation."

"Nathan and Kate. Is that so?"

"It is. And it was Nathan I saw at Lichwood's today, with a new partner I don't know."

"And Jon Pilgrim?"

"No, he wasn't there."

"Pity," she mused and seemed to lose herself in a reverie for a moment. Did she like this Jon Pilgrim? Interesting.

Her phone rang, and she snatched it up. "It's me." Someone spoke on the other end of the line, and Ariadne nodded. After a few moments, she ended the call and placed the phone back on the table, taking a moment to herself as she gazed into the middle distance, contemplating something.

After a while, Scott began to wonder if she'd forgotten he was there. He shuffled on the spot and coughed.

Her eyes flicked up to him, and then she smiled. "Thank you for letting me know about Mr Lichwood, Scott. You were right. He is dead. Murdered, in fact, shot in the head. Your contact was right."

"Good to know," Scott replied, making a mental note to thank his source once he had a moment.

"This is a valuable piece of information and could be very profitable." She got up from her seat and stepped out from behind her desk, her easy stride making her look like some kind of panther, stalking its prey. Ariadne had a way of holding herself, of moving and looking at him, that captivated Scott. He couldn't pull his eyes away as her hips swung back and forth beneath her fitted skirt, while her heels clicked on the hard floor.

His mind went to carnal places as he imagined grabbing her, pulling her in, and taking her there and then over the desk. She was a curvy woman, and her clothes served to accentuate her features and show them off. He tried to remain professional, but his eyes betrayed him as he briefly looked her up and down before silently scolding himself for it.

Despite his fantasies, though, the reality was that he was totally at her mercy. Frozen to the spot as she approached like an apex predator, he felt like a bug beneath her magnifying glass, waiting for her to sear another limb off.

She was alluring and sexy, but also powerful and dangerous, and not to be trifled with. Moving close, she placed a hand on his chest, leant in and looked at him sideways. He could hear her breathing and watching in fascination as the light caught on her glossy lipstick.

"I'd like you to keep me informed of anything you learn about this case going forward, Scott," she purred. The way she said his name, suggested things... Naughty things. "You've done well, and I will be sure to reward you."

"Thank you," he gasped, doing his best to keep his composure. Not an easy task when it came to Ariadne. There was something about the woman that both aroused him and set his teeth on edge. It was an intoxicating cocktail.

"Off you pop now, I have work to do."

Scott's head bobbed up and down, aware that he probably looked like a dutiful puppy. "Of course. Thank you."

"My pleasure."

11

"He's ready for us?" Nathan asked over the phone to the officer downstairs.

"He is," the voice said at the end of the line.

"Excellent, thank you," Nathan replied and hung up, pleased. Bringing Lester Harris in had been easier and less painful than he'd thought it might be. He was exactly where his file said he would be, and he came in without any fuss or trouble, according to the officers who'd picked him up a short time ago. Not only that, but his solicitor had arrived in short order, and they'd only really had a fifteen-minute chat before his phone had rung to let him know Lester was ready for them.

Maybe things were improving and Lester might provide them with some information that would lead them to Terry.

Of course, this was no doubt going to be the point where things started to go awry, and his day turned to shit, but for the moment, it was nice to have a sense of hope about the case.

Replacing the receiver of his desk phone, he looked at Ellie, who was also on a call.

She looked bored and shrugged as she met his gaze. "I'm still on hold."

"Of course you are." Nathan noticed an email alert on his screen. Opening it, he saw it had come from the tech team who'd been going through the security footage from the Lichwood estate. There was a link to a video, and several attached screenshots, which Nathan opened one by one.

As the first image filled the screen, he felt the last of the uncertainty fall from his shoulders. He saw the group of people in dark clothing walking through the mansion's entrance hall. They were led by a large bald man that Nathan recognised right away.

It was Terry Sims. The Dragon. The thug and killer he'd crossed paths with several times in his life, and he was up to his old tricks again. The other images showed one of his team shooting the girl, and another was of Terry, holding his gun to Elden's head. The final image was of Terry watching one of his crew spray painting the wall with the dragon tag.

While it felt good to be right about it being Terry, that feeling was outweighed by the troubling feelings he got from knowing that this killer from his past was out there again, causing havoc once more. He stared into that cold, unfeeling face on the screen and knew he had to do something soon. Terry had been a thorn in his side for too long now. They needed to put him away for good this time.

Sitting back, he glanced through the images for a second time, taking care to have a good look at the other people with him, but they all wore masks, hiding their identities. What he could tell, though, was that one of them was probably female, while the rest were male.

Nathan frowned. Was he running with his old crew from the Abban case? He had a woman on his team back then too. If he was, that tallied up with what he and Kate already knew; that the two surviving members of his team had gone missing around the time of Terry's escape from prison.

"And he can't do any sooner?" he heard Ellie ask. "This is a matter of urgency, you understand, his life could be in danger... No, I know that. I realise that... I'm sure they're very good, yes... Right, okay then. Okay. That sounds good. Thank you. We'll be there. Thanks. Bye."

She hung up and stared at her phone for a moment pulling a face and screwing up her mouth in consternation.

"You're about to ruin my good mood, aren't you," Nathan said.

Ellie rolled her eyes and sighed heavily. "I finally got through to Grey's assistant, but he can't see us until tomorrow. He's just too busy."

"Too busy? Christ, these entitled fools. His life is at risk, and he can't spare us a few minutes of his time?"

Ellie gave him a shrug. "Apparently not."

Nathan shook his head in frustration as he recalled similar brush-offs from other wealthy, powerful people through the years who thought themselves above the law, or at least too rich to be bothered with helping the police with anything. In his experience, they were often the same people who had their own dodgy schemes going on behind the scenes too.

"Alright," Nathan said. "When are we meeting him?"

"In the morning at 10 am, but the man on the phone warned me that if Grey was busy, we might have a bit of a wait or even have to postpone the meeting for another day."

"We're just a joke to people like him."

"You've had to deal with people like them before, I take it."

"Too many times," Nathan replied. "You did say to him that we have a credible threat to his life, right?"

"I did. The man seemed to think that Grey's security was up to the job of protecting him until tomorrow."

"I hope so."

"What about you? You seemed positively happy before I told you about my phone call."

"That's because I was," he admitted. "Well, firstly, I've just had it confirmed that we're after Terry Sims. I had some security images come through, showing the house invasion."

"Excellent. So Terry wasn't hiding his face?"

"No. He went in bold as brass, showing the world his face, and murdered Elden." It fit Terry's M.O. to do that though. As far as Nathan was aware, he'd never hidden his face before and relied on the silence of the criminal community and the excellent lawyers he was granted by the men he worked for. But hopefully, this time, it would be his downfall. If they could catch him.

"Ballsy," Ellie agreed.

"Also, Lester is downstairs, and he's ready to speak to us."

"Already? My, that was quick."

"I know."

"No wonder you were pleased," Ellie remarked.

"So, what do we have on Lester?"

"Well..." Ellie swung back to the computer. "He was done on breaking and entering and got a few years for it. Embezzlement too. It seems like he's a bit of a computer whiz. But most recently, he's been charged with GBH and ABH which is what he was in for when he met Terry. This was his longest stretch."

"Okay, so he's a violent man with loose morals and skills that might be useful to someone like Terry," Nathan surmised, seeing why Terry might be interested in the man.

"That's about the long and short of it, yes. Sounds like the perfect recruit for Terry's crew."

"Doesn't he just. Alright, let's go and have a chat and see what he has to say for himself."

"Sir." Ellie got up from her desk and followed him across the room towards the stairs. As they approached, she cleared her throat. "I hope I didn't upset Kate earlier."

Nathan smiled as he started down the stairs. "I very much doubt it. She's a tough one."

"Sounds like she's had it rough, though."

"She's been through a lot, where Abban's concerned. That's for sure. We both have, actually." The series of murders that he and Kate had investigated when they were partners were certainly some of the most gruesome that he'd come across. The eventual revelation that there was a wealthy organisation behind it all only confirmed some of the suspicions he'd held over the years.

Part of him had felt vindicated that his suspicions had been right all along. But the knowledge had a dark side to it, as he wondered how far the influence of the group extended. Had his own demotion been in some way influenced by these wealthy, powerful people and designed to shut him up and stop him from investigating them? He'd never really know, especially now that Terry seemed to be assassinating the very people who might have arranged it.

They had to move quickly to stop Terry and bring him to justice before anyone else got hurt. If they didn't, more innocents like the woman at Elden's house could be caught in the crossfire, and although he didn't mourn the passing of people like Elden, they did have information that Nathan was keen to get his hands on. But this group was slippery, and just when you thought you had a good grip on them, they'd slither back into the shadows, and you'd have to start from scratch again.

This time, he hoped it would be different, but it was perhaps a slim hope, and one he'd need to let go of at some point.

Reaching the interview rooms, they were shown to the one with Lester in it and found him sitting behind the well-worn desk with his lawyer beside him. Lester chewed his cheek as Nathan walked in, and Ellie followed.

"Lester Harris, right?" Nathan began. He recognised him from his mugshot but chose to confirm it anyway.

"That's right," Lester replied, slumped into the chair which was turned more towards his solicitor than to Ellie and himself. "That's my name. Don't wear it out."

"Lester has served his time in jail for his crimes," his lawyer said, leaning forward. "So we're curious to know why you felt the need to bring him in, when he has done nothing wrong."

"I was getting to that," Nathan replied, sounding a little more stern than he had intended. "I am well aware that there have been no reports against Lester since his release, which is commendable. However, before we go any further, I just need to set this recording." Nathan hit the record button on the DIR and proceeded to introduce everyone.

With that done, he leant in and fixed Lester with his gaze. "We need to talk to you, about certain events that took place within High Down Prison."

"Like what? You do what you have to survive in there, you know."

"I agree, prison life is tough," Nathan replied. "Sometimes people get hurt because there might be a rivalry between two prisoners, and sometimes those prisoners are kept away from each other for their own safety."

Lester shrugged. "So. So what? What am I meant to have done?"

"This needs to go somewhere, Detective," the lawyer added.

"Wind your neck in," Nathan said, annoyed by the nerve of the guy. "You knew Abban Devlin and Terry Sims, right?"

"I knew a lot of people, detective," Lester replied.

"I think you'd remember Terry, and maybe Abban too. Especially after what Terry did to him."

"And that concerns me, how?"

"We were contacted by the prison a short time ago and informed that they have discovered that Terry was granted access to Abban at least partially by your actions. Now, these two men were being kept apart because Terry's anger towards Abban was well known, but because you helped bring them together, Abban is in a critical condition and Terry has escaped."

"And you think that's all down to me, do you?"

"Do you deny it?" It was a rhetorical question because he was quite sure that Lester would never admit to such a thing.

"Of course I do. I didn't do anything."

"But you knew Abban, and you knew Terry."

"I don't know. Maybe. But so what, that's not a crime, is it?"

"Having friends is not a crime, no. But helping someone seriously injure someone else, well, that is."

"I'd like to see what proof you have of this because this is bull shit. I ain't helped either of them two do anything, alright?"

"But you were in prison for breaking and entering, and GBH, correct?"

"Yeah."

"So you know how to open locked doors, right?"

"Yeah. You turn a key, duh!"

Nathan sighed and fixed him with a level stare. "Don't play silly buggers with me, Mr Harris. You know what I mean."

"Actually, I don't. All I did in that prison is survive, taking one day at a time, like everyone else. I didn't assist anyone in any kind of attack."

"I wish I could say I believe you, Lester, but I really don't. Not at all."

Lester grunted, crossed his arms and sat back, sticking his bottom lip out in a show of defiance that reminded Nathan of a child. He wasn't going to admit to anything, and it didn't look like there was much he could do right now. He needed to evaluate the evidence that the prison had on him. The thing was, if there were any holes in it, any at all, it would be pulled apart by any reasonably competent lawyer, and this would go nowhere.

It was frustrating, but there was little he could do right now other than push on and see what he could wring out of all this.

With a frown, Nathan changed tack. "So, what's Terry up to now?"

Lester pulled a face. "How should I know?"

"You're mates, and you're both out of the clink, so I figured you'd meet up."

Lester smirked. "Yeah, whatever dude. I'm going straight. I don't want anything to do with Terry. He's a thug."

"Is he?"

"Yeah. I've got no stake in whatever crazy plan he's got going on."

"Crazy plan? What crazy plan is that?"

Lester held Nathan's gaze for a moment, assessing him and probably thinking about his answer. He seemed to sense the trap that Nathan had manoeuvred him towards. "Dunno. But if he's attacked this guy you mentioned and broke out of prison, I assume there's a reason for it. You don't do that for shits and giggles."

"Do you not?"

"Well, I wouldn't. But like I said, I've got nothing to do with the twat. He can go fuck himself, for all I care."

"You see, it's funny because I think you'd be quite a valuable asset to him. With your skills, you could help him get what he wants."

"And what's that?"

"You tell me," Nathan goaded.

"Oh, you're good. I'll give you that," Lester said, waving a finger at Nathan as a grin spread across his face. "You've got that patter down, man. You really do. But it won't work on me, cos I ain't done nothing wrong. I've got nothing to do with Terry. You've got the wrong man. Sounds like Terry's done something to get you all worked up though. What's he done? Has he hurt someone? Killed someone?"

Nathan ignored the questions. "So you're saying you have no idea where he is, or what he's up to?"

"Nope. So, if we're done here, I think I'd quite like to fuck off out of here and get myself some dinner. Is that alright with you, guv?"

Nathan shrugged. "You're not under arrest, Mr Harris, so you're free to leave."

Lester stood up, knocking his chair back, and stretched. "Wicked." A huge shit-eating grin spread over his face as he placed his hands on his hips. "Well, this has been fun."

Nathan was also on his feet. "Thank you for coming in, Mr Harris."

"My pleasure, man. My pleasure." Lester turned to Ellie. "I don't think I got to say hello to you, though, young lady. Miss Mizaki, was it?"

"Thank you for coming in, Mr Harris," Ellie said, without missing a beat. She was all business.

"If you'd like to come this way," Nathan urged, diverting his attention away from her. He walked Lester out into the corridor, guiding him towards the exit.

"Well, hello there," Lester said, ahead of him.

Nathan looked past him to see Kate approaching from the other direction, frowning at Lester.

"Kate, isn't it? Kate O'Connell?" Lester added.

Kate paused. "Sorry, do I know you?"

"No. I've just heard of you," Lester replied.

"How?" Nathan asked, suddenly curious.

Lester turned to him and smiled. "Do you think we don't talk, Detective? We have endless days in prison with nothing to do other than talk with people you lot have put away. And guess what, this Irish redhead here kinda stands out." Lester turned back to Kate. "You've made quite the impression, you know."

Kate's eyes flicked back and forth between Nathan and Lester, looking ever more uncomfortable. "I'm flattered, I'm sure."

He wasn't sure what that was all about, and other than having a professional curiosity, he had no desire to know what creeps like Lester talked about in the long hours they shared locked up. Bored of Lester's antics, Nathan decided to end it before he offended anyone else. "Right, that's enough out of you," Nathan said, and ushered Lester towards the exit, leaving Kate to go about her business.

Within moments, Lester was gone, and so was his lawyer, leaving Nathan and Ellie in the lobby of Horsley Station.

"Well, that was weird," Ellie said.

"You're not kidding."

12

Jon wandered into the corridor, where the doors to the station's various interview rooms lined the left-hand wall, to find Kate waiting for him.

She was looking past him, further up the corridor to the other exit at the end with a curious look on her face. Jon followed her gaze, but saw only a closed door.

"What's up?" he asked, approaching her.

"Oh, nothing. I've just had a strange encounter with someone that Nathan was questioning."

"Oh?" Jon glanced back up the hallway, but there was still no one there. "Who was that?"

"I have no idea. But he said he knew me from talking to other inmates at the prison."

"Really? Hmm." It was a strange feeling, knowing that the people they had arrested were talking about them while they were locked up. But he guessed it was only natural. They might be criminals, but they were also just human, like everyone else.

"He said I stood out."

"I don't know about that, but you are a beautiful woman."

Kate fixed him with an incredulous scowl and raised an eyebrow. "And what the hell are you after?"

"Nothing, just flattering you with a compliment."

"Hmm, Is that right? Why? Do you want one in return?"

"They're always nice to get," Jon answered with a grin, goading her, feeling like he wanted to raise the mood. "Am I not allowed to offer you a compliment?"

"Of course you are..."

"Well then, let's leave it at that. So, what have you got for me? Anything new?"

"You're after something, I know it. But yeah, okay. I'll leave it there," Kate answered, and shifted her weight to the other foot. "So, I've been looking into Jess's mother, Cathy, and the missing person's case that was filed six years ago when she went missing. It was investigated at the time, but the case didn't really come to any kind of satisfactory conclusion and Cathy herself was never found. It appears that she left the house in the early hours while Mickey and the children were asleep. She even left a note for Henry and Jess, apologising for leaving them without warning. But it seems like living with Mickey just became too much for her to bear, and she left. She does say, in the note, that she would return for the kids, but she never did. Also, friends of hers have never heard from her, from that date."

"Okay. I take it Mickey was investigated?"

"He was, but there was no solid evidence linking him to her disappearance. According to him, he was sleeping in their bed the whole night, and only noticed her disappearance the following morning."

"When did the police get involved?"

"According to the case files, Mickey went out looking for her, checking with friends and driving around, and it was only later that day that the police were called in."

Jon sighed as he considered the facts. "So if we assume that Mickey killed her during the night, he could have disposed of the body that night and returned to bed, or even the next day when he was supposedly out searching for her."

Kate shrugged. "Yep and the investigating detectives at the time knew that and noted it in the files. But there was no proof."

"Did they look into Cathy's friends?"

"They did. It seems like Cathy was unhappy in the relationship for some time and had been planning to leave Mickey for a while, putting plans in place. Her closest friends knew she was planning to sneak out in the night and helped out when they could. But then she just disappeared."

"Alright. But if we take the stance of Mickey being innocent until proven guilty, it is plausible that Cathy is out there somewhere. Perhaps she did leave him and head out into the world. She could have gone abroad for all we know, and maybe something happened to her once she'd left him."

"Anything's possible at this point," Kate agreed. "I'm looking into it still."

"Good. Okay." Jon glanced at the door closest to them. "I'm right in thinking we have Henry, Jess's brother in there?"

Kate gave him a nod as she turned towards the nearby interview room. "Correct. He's in there with his legal representative."

"Is he ready for us?"

"Yeah. I don't think he was thrilled to be dragged in, though."

"I'd expect nothing less. Alright then, let's head inside." He opened the nearest door and found a pissed off young man, similar in age to Jess, sitting beside his solicitor, his arms crossed and his mouth tightly shut.

"Good evening, Henry," Jon started. "I'm Detective Pilgrim, and this is Detective O'Connell." He glanced across to the solicitor and gave her a nod too.

The duty solicitor smiled up at him. He recognised Ana Allen from Marshall and Edwards Solicitors in Guildford. She was a regular face around the station.

"Ana," Jon said. "Good to see you."

Henry glanced between her and Jon. "You know this clown?" Henry asked her.

Ana fixed him with a look. "As I've explained, I'm your duty solicitor, and I've represented a lot of people in this station."

"Oh, yeah... course..." Henry replied, calming down.

"I'm sorry for your loss," Kate said as she took her seat.

"Thanks," Henry muttered, shifting uncomfortably in his seat. Jon could see the pain in his eyes, despite the bravado he was displaying. He gave Kate an approving glance for showing this young man a human face to the police.

"Were you and Jess close?"

Henry shrugged. "Dunno. Not really."

"Well, we're sorry all the same. We'd be happy to arrange some help for you, if you're interested?"

"No, thanks. Let's get this over with, shall we?"

"You don't have to be here, Henry. You're not under arrest."

"I know."

He was acting very sullen, with his arms crossed. He was refusing to look at them too, preferring to stare at the table than look at him or Kate. His guard was up.

"We're going to find who did this to your sister," Jon said.

The young man grunted.

"Right, well, let's get this started, shall we?" Jon continued and set the recorder going before introducing everyone in the room for the benefit of the audio recording.

"What can you tell me about your relationship with your sister?" Jon asked.

"She was alright, I suppose."

"Just alright?"

"Yeah."

"So, you got along and were friendly, then, I take it. Like most siblings."

"Yeah."

"Were there any disagreements between you? Was there anything about her that you didn't like?"

"Not really."

Jon frowned, annoyed at the kid's curt answers. It was already feeling like trying to get blood out of a stone. He understood why, though. The young man had been through several encounters with the police in his life, and already had an impressive criminal record. It was only natural that he viewed the police with distrust and maybe even hate. He was used to clamming up and saying nothing while around officers like him and Kate.

Adjusting his position, Jon decided to try another line of questioning.

"What about her job? You knew about that, didn't you? The photos she took of herself and posted online?"

"Yeah."

"And what did you think about that?"

"Whatever, man. She can do whatever she likes. She's a grown woman, right? Ain't nothing I could say to stop her, was there? She does what she wants."

"Even if it causes upset?"

"Maybe."

"Did it upset you?" It clearly did from the expression on the kid's face, and the way he held himself.

"A bit."

"Just a bit?" He wanted the kid to open himself up more. He was a suspect, like his dad, but he was also a victim. His sister had been murdered, and ultimately, he and Kate just wanted to find the killer. He had to try and make him see that.

"Look man, I'm not interested in looking at her pictures. They're for cucks and creeps, not me."

Jon raised an eyebrow at his comment. It gave him an insight into what Henry thought of the people who were fans of Jess and what she did, and it wasn't a favourable view at all. "So you didn't like what she was doing?"

"Nah. Not really."

"Did it upset you?"

"I ain't crying over it, if that's what you're asking, no. It's her life. She could do whatever she wanted with it. Doesn't mean I have to like it, though. Why? You think I killed her or some shit?"

"We're just trying to get a handle on the family dynamic," Kate explained. "We're not accusing you of anything."

Yet, Jon mused silently to himself.

"Yeah, right. I know what you're like," Henry said, and Jon felt sure he heard him whisper something like 'fuckin' pigs' under his breath, showing Jon that they had not yet broken through to him. They had some work to do.

"Tell me about your dad," Jon said, changing the subject. "Do you have a better relationship with him?"

"I don't know. I guess. I always saw him more often than Jess, for sure. She was hardly around, but she didn't really get on with my dad. Not like I did. She was more friendly with my mum."

Jon nodded as Henry spoke, pleased that the young man had opened up to them a little. "And your dad, I understand that he didn't like Jess's chosen profession, either?"

Henry slumped again. "No, not really. He wasn't a fan."

"I think that's putting it mildly."

Henry sneered at him. "Seems like you know my family better than I do. So if you know all this, why you asking me? Oh, you think my dad killed her, do you? Is that it? Fuck off, he wouldn't do that."

"Are you sure?"

"Your mother disappeared six years ago," Kate suggested, making it clear that they wondered if there might be a link there.

"And you think he offed her too, do you? What utter crap. He didn't kill Mum. She left us for fuck knows what reason. She was probably banging some other guy for all I know. But whatever. Fuck her. She wasn't interested in me or Dad. She was only interested in Jess. Well, now she's got her all to herself, ain't she? And good riddance to 'em."

"She left you a note, didn't she, when she left?"

"What *is* all this man? I ain't answering these dumb questions."

"Do you remember what the note said?"

Henry sighed. "No comment."

Jon frowned, annoyed that he'd lost him just when he was starting to open up. It was interesting to see the different perspectives on the disappearance of Henry and Jess's mother. According to her boyfriend, Jess had been close to her mother, who supported her in her burgeoning modelling career. And it seemed like Jess believed that her father had something to do with Cathy's disappearance. But Henry believed differently and seemed to side with his father in thinking that Cathy abandoned them.

Either could be right at this point, but what did this mean for Jess's murder? Were they barking up the wrong tree by looking at Jess's family? Maybe this was done by an outside party after all.

"Do you know anyone who might do this?" Kate asked him. "Was there anyone you were aware of that hated Jess enough to kill her? Anyone at all?"

Henry chewed his lip as he listened to Kate speak. He closed his eyes and looked away.

"We're just trying to find out who murdered your sister," Kate continued. "And we need your help to do it. I'm sorry if the questions make you... uncomfortable, but we need to look at all the angles. So if you know something that might help us, then please, tell us. I'm sure you don't want your sister's death to go unavenged, no matter what you thought of her job."

Henry sighed again and stared at the floor.

"You want us to find her killer, don't you?" Kate continued.

"Yes, I do," he said finally. "It's true, I didn't like what she did. It was embarrassing when my mates found out. They were always going on about it, pissing me off about my so-called 'slut sister'. It was fucking humiliating, but she didn't seem to care."

"Why do you think that?"

"Because she didn't stop," Henry replied with venom in his words. "She just kept on doing it, and my mates kept trying to show me what she was posting. But I didn't want to see that. She's my fucking sister."

"I understand," Kate said. "Of course, you didn't. She was your sister and you didn't like to see her flaunting herself to strangers. There's nothing embarrassing in caring for your family. You have every right to be angry and frustrated, especially now. Remember, we're on your sister's side with this, we want to find out who did this to her. If you want that too, then we need your help."

"I know..."

"Who do you think killed her?" Kate asked. The question shot out of the blue, designed to take him off guard and hopefully get an answer that was perhaps a little more enlightening.

"Probably one of those bloody stalkers."

Stalkers again, Jon mused. He'd said the same thing that his father had.

"Did you know of any in particular?" Jon asked.

"Not really. She told me in the early days about some of the disgusting messages she would get from some of her so-called fans. It was gross. They'd threaten to rape her or kill her, or both. They went into a lot of detail, too."

"So you don't remember any names?" Kate replied.

"No, sorry. We've not been close in recent years, so we've not really talked about it."

"That's fine," Kate said.

"Your dad believed it was a stalker too," Jon added.

"Yeah," Henry answered. "We've spoken about it before."

"And you both came to the same conclusion?" Jon enquired.

"Yeah. What's wrong with that?"

"Nothing's wrong with it."

"Yeah, right. Fuck off. Why don't you leave me alone and go hunting for some of those sickos."

"As my colleague said, we need to look at it from all angles, and unfortunately, you do have a criminal record for violent crime. You've hurt people. So surely you can understand why we need to take that into account."

"I wouldn't hurt my sister."

"I hope that's true, but in my experience, we tend to hurt the people closest to us."

Henry looked tired as he sighed and slumped in his chair. "I guess you'd know...."

"Unfortunately, yes, I would," Jon agreed, thinking back over the years of doing this job and the horrors that some people would inflict on those closest to them. It was a nightmare that he and his fellow detectives got to experience every day and relive night after night.

13

Manoeuvring the car slowly, with care, Grey turned the vehicle into his private parking bay and switched off the engine. Its deep throaty rumble died, and the lights on the dash faded.

Satisfied, he opened the driver's side scissor-door and climbed out. Nearby, an immaculately dressed young man waited patiently with a smile.

"Mr Davison, would you like me to put the cover on your car?"

"Hey, Stefan. Yeah, thanks. That would be great."

"Are you on your own, tonight?"

"Afraid so," he shrugged, finding it amusing that the young man knew him well enough to make the comment, and realise that he often returned home with a lady friend on his arm. But not tonight. "You know me too well."

"Sorry, sir. I didn't mean..."

Grey raised a hand. "Ah-ah. Don't worry about it. It's fine," he replied, closing the car door and locking it. He watched as Stefan pulled the cover from storage and set to work. It almost felt like sacrilege to hide his Lamborghini's bright green paintwork from the world, but he knew better than to leave his car on show, even inside this exclusive parking area.

"Busy night?" Grey asked, glancing around the small cordoned off parking area reserved for the residents who lived on the top few floors.

"Somewhat. I've picked up a few good tips already." Stefan smiled.

Grey smiled to himself, noting the clever comment that both reminded him to tip the young man, as well as breed a sense of competition and get a higher tip. The kid was smart. "I see." He reached into his pocket and pulled out his billfold. Sliding a couple of fifties from it, he held them out to Stefan. "Here you go."

"Thank you, sir," the young man replied. "You're very generous."

"You know I appreciate diligent workers," Grey said. He must have tipped Stefan thousands by now, over the months he'd been working here. But it was nothing in the grand scheme of things. The kid was a great worker and always treated him with respect. He deserved a little bonus here and there.

Excusing himself, Grey wandered over to the exclusive elevators in the corner, watched over by one of the building's security guards, and found a lift waiting for him. "Evening,"

Grey muttered to the guard, a new employee who he'd not seen before.

"Good evening, sir," the guard replied. "Hope you had a great night."

Grey gave him a brief side-eye. "It's alright, I suppose."

Stepping inside, he tapped the button for his floor and pulled his phone out as the box rose out of the basement towards the upper levels.

Moments later, he made his way along the corridor to his luxury penthouse apartment, thinking about his day at work and the meetings and appointments coming up. Today had been taken up, for the most part, with one long meeting with an important client. There'd been a few stressful points for his team, but in the end, an agreement had been reached and a plan going forward was formulated.

Grey himself hadn't been terribly concerned and was more dedicated to making the deal work for the company, but his team had been a little more invested, which was only natural.

As he wandered along the short hallway, his phone vibrated with an incoming call. Plucking it out of his pocket, he recognised his PA's name on the screen and answered it. "Anthony, what's up? Sorry I didn't check in with you before I left the office."

"That's okay, Mr Davison. I just wanted to make sure everything went well today? I know it was an important meeting."

Another worried employee, he mused. "It went great. I think they're on board with us, so no need to worry."

"I wasn't worried, sir," Anthony replied.

"Good man. Well, if that's all…?"

"Actually, there was one other thing. I had a call from the police today."

Grey slowed at the mention of the police. "Oh, really?"

"Yes. A Detective Mizaki. She seemed to think that your life was in danger, sir, and requested a meeting at your earliest convenience. I've booked it in for tomorrow. I know how important today's meeting was for you."

One of his PA's main jobs was to act as a filter and limit the people who had access to him, and he'd done his job well. "Good work. Did she say anything else? Such as what this threat might be?"

"No, sir. She didn't want to say too much, only that they were aware of a credible threat to your life."

"Hmm, okay."

"Should we be unduly concerned?"

"No, I don't think so, Tony. I'm sure it's nothing."

"I hope so. The meeting will be in your office, as usual."

"Perfect. Anything else?"

"Nothing that can't wait until tomorrow, sir."

"Great. I'll see you tomorrow." Ending the call, Grey approached his front door, unlocked it, and made his way inside, making sure to lock it securely behind him.

A credible threat, Grey mused to himself, wondering what, exactly, it might be. He was no stranger to people hating him and had received more than his fair share of death threats over the years. But that seemed to be an occupational hazard when it came to people who were as wealthy as he was. He was well aware of others in a similar financial position to him, who'd had similar threats, almost daily. Then there were those who were always trying to sue him and take his money. It was almost comical how regularly these things happened. So much so that he had a law firm on a retainer, who dealt with all his legal troubles.

But he had to admit, having a detective call him directly was a new one.

With a sigh, he let the worry fade. He was well protected in here with the security guards, reinforced door, and deadbolts.

He wandered through to his living room and made for the drinks cabinet, where he poured himself a scotch and took a moment to gaze out over the city at night. Lit up by hundreds of thousands of lights, it was like a glittering starfield of yellows, reds and oranges twinkling in the night, overwhelming the actual stars up above.

It was a shame he hadn't picked up a girl from a club on his way back, someone to have some fun and share the view with. Having sex here on the couch at night, surrounded by the city lights, was always glorious.

Grey threw back the scotch and returned the glass to the sideboard before he wandered over to his desk and opened up his laptop.

Immediately, an alert popped up on the screen. It was a message sent through a private channel set-up by Elden Lichwood. It was from his friend's lawyers.

Frowning, Grey opened the message. "To Mr Davison. We regret to inform you that Elden Lichwood was unfortunately murdered in the early hours of last night. It appears that he was executed, and we believe that the perpetrator might pose a threat to you as well. We advise that you take all precautions necessary to protect yourself. We wish you all the best. Thank you."

Grey blinked as he re-read the message to check he wasn't imagining things. Elden was dead? Holy shit. What the hell was going on?

Sitting back, he remembered the message his PA gave him about the call from the police. Looking up, he realised how alone he was up here, and felt suddenly vulnerable. Perhaps there was more to this new threat to his life than the usual letters and anonymous emails he got most days from people who believed he should be killed in some horrific manner.

Gazing around the silent apartment, he peered into the shadows, momentarily terrified that he'd find a face there, staring back at him, but there was none, and he shook his head in exasperation.

He was being an idiot... or was he? He did his best to keep his address out of the papers and such, but it wouldn't be exactly difficult for someone to find out where he lived. Plenty of people knew he lived here, in London.

Glancing over at the hallway that led to the front door, he started wondering how solid it was. Would it really keep him safe? Was that guard downstairs really up to stopping an assassin who wanted to reach him?

Who was the guy, anyway? He'd not seen that guard before. Was he new? Or was he a threat? A lookout, waiting to see when he returned?

Putting his head in his hands, he rubbed his tired eyes and took a moment to get a hold of himself. He was being silly. These kinds of thoughts didn't achieve anything. Instead, he needed to think a little more practically.

He turned and looked out over the city, wondering where he could go that was more secure than here? Maybe he should just take a room in a random hotel under a fake name and pay in cash. He could take one of his less conspicuous cars or even borrow someone else's for the night.

As he worked through his options, he noticed movement in the reflection of the glass and felt a shiver pass down his spine. As terror flooded his system, he jumped up and turned.

A group of men, led by a large bald man he'd seen pictures of, but never met, strode into his apartment having somehow bypassed his locked front door. For a moment, Grey was rooted to the spot as a deep, guttural fear flooded his system. For what felt like an age, he couldn't quite wrap his head around what was going on. Who were these men and what were they doing in his home?

"Mr Davison," the lead man called out, and it was at that moment that he spotted the gun he was holding. The terror in his gut suddenly gripped him. Without thinking, Grey bolted left. He sprinted across his open plan living space, running for the corridors and rooms to the left of the thugs. If he could just get into one of those rooms and lock it, maybe he could call security or something?

As he ran, he heard the man call out. "Get him."

Grey charged into the hallway and skidded to a stop at his bedroom door, for a moment he considered diving inside. Could he lock it?

No, there wasn't a lock on that door. Damn it. Grey lunged deeper into the corridor, but stopped and pulled back, looking across his bedroom again to the shelf behind his bed. Displayed on a rack, gleaming in the half light, was a beautiful Samurai Sword.

A weapon.

As the sound of thundering feet grew louder, Grey ran into the room with the thugs just metres behind him. He jumped onto the bed, grabbed the blade and went to draw it.

He was tackled a half second later and knocked off his feet. Grey roared as he fought against the press of bodies and hands ripping the sword away before they pinned him to the bed.

He was left sprawled on his back, his feet by the pillows and his head hanging off the end of the bed, cringing as the large bald man strode easily into the room and raised the gun. He rested the muzzle against Grey's forehead.

"Mr Davison, thank you for the moment of excitement. Are we going to have any further trouble from you?"

Grey gave his head a brief shake. "No, Terry." He knew this man, mainly by reputation, and the occasional photo. He was a thug, a killer that Abban liked to use, as well as some of the other members of the organisation. He was a blunt instrument, but he'd been useful until Abban got him locked up.

Now he was out, and it looked like he was out for revenge.

"So, you know my name."

"I know who you are." Grey noted that Terry's crew were tying him to the bed, leaving him defenceless.

"Good, then you know why I'm here."

"I didn't use you."

"I don't give a shit. You were in it with the others, and that makes you just as guilty. Besides, you have something that might be useful to me." Terry looked left at the much thinner man who stood to one side holding a laptop. "Ready?"

"Uh, yeah, hold on."

"This better work, Lester."

"It will." The man seemed to grimace at the use of his name, and glanced at Grey, before turning to a table and chair where he set up the laptop and started clicking and typing.

"It better."

"I just need some information, and then I can get to work."

"Make it quick. Just drain his accounts."

Lester gave Terry a look. "Don't be an idiot..."

"What!"

"Sorry, I mean, I can't just make one massive transfer, it'll get flagged and then we'll have the banks and the fraud team to deal with. We've got to be smart about this."

"D, d, do… Do you want… m, money?" Grey stammered. "You can have money."

Terry looked back at him and then lunged. Pain exploded through Grey's gut as Terry punched him. "Shut up." Terry turned back to Lester. "This was your idea; you came to me."

"And I've already got you up here without alerting security, haven't I, so go with me on this, yeah? And don't worry, we'll be rich. But I need some login information first."

"Right," Terry said, and then glowered at Grey. "Let's see how cooperative you can be, shall we?"

14

Driving east, out of Guildford, Jon wiped some stubborn sleep from his eye as they moved through the Surrey countryside towards Horsley and another day's work on the SIU. So far, from what he could tell, the killer had not struck again. There'd been no messages from the night shift, and no reports on the news this morning over breakfast.

Jon counted his blessings about that. No one else deserved to suffer the same fate that Jess had. He only hoped that they found the killer before he managed to strike again.

"You look tired," Kate said, leaning back in her seat beside him and fixing him with a keen stare. He felt like he was being examined. But it was true, he was tired. His mind had been going over the facts of the case all night, over and over, trying to see if there was another angle on it. They'd not exhausted their lines of enquiry yet, though.

But that wasn't the only thing that had kept him awake.

"Yeah, that's because I am. Didn't sleep well at all."

"Why not?"

"I just couldn't turn my brain off," he explained.

"The case?"

"Yeah, other stuff too."

"Like what?"

Feeling unsure about how to approach this, he didn't want to offend her or scare her off, but he also wanted to know more. He wanted to know what she was thinking and where her head was at.

"Oh, a few things, but..."

"But, what?" He could hear the curiosity in her voice.

"Well, I was wondering if you were serious about wanting to move in with me?"

"Oh," she replied, surprised. "Really? You were thinking about that?"

"Yeah, and police stuff too. So, not just that. I hope you don't mind me asking?"

"No, I don't mind."

"So, what do you think?"

"I don't know, really. I mean, the thought had crossed my mind, but I've been a little distracted by the case."

"Yeah. Me too."

"I guess, I suppose, I am interested. But I was joking when I mentioned it yesterday morning. I wasn't being serious."

"I guessed," Jon answered. He'd realised that, but he felt sure that she wouldn't have mentioned it if it hadn't been on her mind, at least in a small way. Maybe he was wrong, but he took that joke to mean something.

"I need to have a think about it," she replied. "It would mean me selling my place."

"It would."

"I don't know. I'm not sure I have the headspace to deal with that today, while all this stuff at work is going on. Can you let me think on it for a while, and I'm not saying no."

"Of course, that's fine. No rush."

"I mean, I like the idea. I do. I love you, Jon. But that would be a big step, and it's not something I'd want to rush into without putting some serious thought into it. Also, are you sure you're ready?"

Jon shrugged. "I dunno. I think, yeah, maybe. I think so."

"Alright then. Leave it with me."

Jon gave her a nod. "Okay."

Kate fell silent after that, so to fill the void, Jon turned the radio on as he pushed through the wintery scenes that slid by all around them. They were most of the way there when the news came on, and there was a report about a local businessman who'd been found dead in his home yesterday.

The reporter said that their name had yet to be released, but Jon felt certain this would be Elden Lichwood. It was surprising to hear this being reported, given that yesterday this was being blocked by Elden's lawyers. He doubted that this radio station had gone rogue and was the first to report it, which meant either the lawyers were loosening their grip, or someone had leaked it.

If Jon had to guess, he'd say it was the latter, and they'd been forced into releasing something.

"It was bound to get out eventually," Kate commented.

She was right. It was.

They got into the station a short time later.

The huge brutalist building dominated the quaint countryside landscape in the small village of Horsley. The location was perfect, and right in the middle of the county, giving them good access to all corners of their primary territory.

But the reach of the SIU could go much further when needed due to it being at least partially under the auspices of the National Crime Agency. The Special Investigations Unit needed to be able to operate where ever they needed to, after all.

Once inside the SIU offices, Kate disappeared off to her desk to work on a few things before the morning briefing, while Jon entered his office and booted up his PC.

"Morning, Jon," Nathan said a few moments later, standing at the door and leaning into the room.

"Hi, Nathan. How's things?"

"Looks like it's going to be another eventful day," he replied. Jon looked up and could see the look on Nathan's face. It didn't take much for him to realise what that meant.

"He's struck again, hasn't he."

"Yep," Nathan replied. "We got a call a short time ago from the Met, referring a case over to us. They found Grey Davison's body this morning, and soon linked it to our case."

"The Met? So he was killed in London?"

"In the city, in his penthouse."

"I take it you're going up there?"

"We are," Nathan confirmed.

"Terry's been busy," Jon mused. "Does Kate know?"

"I've not mentioned it, no. I'll leave that to you, Loxley."

Jon smirked at the name.

"What's funny?" Nathan asked.

"Loxley. It's amusing. In fact, it's been funny since you first called me that, but not for the reason you think."

"So, not because it's a well-observed joke, you mean?"

"Yeah, no."

"Why then?" Nathan asked.

"Because I actually know a Detective Loxley, who works in Nottingham." Jon raised an eyebrow and smiled, remembering his days on the Nottinghamshire force fondly. "He used to be on my team, you know."

"Really? You know a Detective Loxley?"

"Yep."

"You're kidding."

"Nope. I'm serious."

"What is he? A DS? DI?"

"Well, it's been a few months now, but he was a DI when I left. Who knows, he might be a DCI by now."

"Good bloke?"

"A little rough around the edges, but he was always a good, solid team member. I should catch up with him sometime, thinking about it."

"Well, I'd better stop calling you by that name, then."

"You certainly should. I think Loxley might have something to say about it if you don't. Anyway, good luck."

"Thanks."

"I'll see you later."

"You will," Nathan replied, and with a wink and a slap of the door frame, disappeared again.

Jon sat back and chewed on his pen. Terry's mission was moving fast and wasn't confined to the local area. How far would this go? How many more people would Terry execute?

Part of him wanted to head into the city with Nathan and assess the crime scene, but that would be a total waste of resources, and they were stretched thin enough as it was. No, he needed to concentrate on Jess and her mystery killer. She was counting on him.

Jon set to work going through the morning's emails and messages, before gathering his things and calling the briefing, bringing the team, minus Nathan and Ellie, together in their incident room.

Walking in to see the whole team waiting for him, Jon placed his files on the table. "Morning campers."

"Hi-di-hi," Rachel replied.

"What?" Dion asked, looking confused.

"Before your time," Jon said with a wistful look. "Right then, I want to hit this case running today. Yesterday we had a day of no answers and just more questions to add to our already huge list. I'd love to have some kind of breakthrough by the end of play, so let's make that happen, yeah?"

There was a chorus of affirmative replies from around the table.

Jon gave them a nod. "Right then. What do we know? I want some good news."

"Well, guv," Dion said, sitting forward. "I've been doing some work on the stalker angle and used what Conrad, the boyfriend, told you about the ones he knew, and it seems he was right, but also unaware of at least one thing that happened."

"Okay. Are we talking about..." Jon leafed through his notes. "...Ken and Ozzy?"

"That's them," Dion confirmed. "Ken Wyndam, and Ozzy. I don't have a surname for him, or photo, and know precious little about Ozzy. Ken however, was a little easier to track down." Dion passed around a photo of Ken. "I got access to Jess's HoundPic inbox and went rooting through her messages to see what I could find. There's a whole massive thread between her and Ken. They've been talking for a long time, right up until, and including the night of her murder, actually."

"So they were friendly?" Kate asked.

"To a certain degree. He seems like a glutton for punishment, actually. She treated him like crap. She was always insulting him and being rude."

"Really?" Jon asked, surprised.

"That was my reaction. It was a curious way to act towards someone who was paying her money every month, so I went back through her message history with him and eventually found the moment when it all changed. It all stems back to an incident a few months ago when Ken actually turned up on her doorstep. He freaked Jess out, and from that day forward, she never treated him the same again."

"He came to her house?!"

"That's right. He somehow worked out where she lived, through a combination of online photos, Google street view, and plain detective work."

"I think we need to get him on the team," Rachel said.

"You're not kidding," Jon agreed. "Christ he's keen. So he knew where she lived. Well, that's a big red flag, if ever there was one. Why did he do that?"

"It seems, from the message thread, that Ken wanted to surprise her and give her some gifts," Dion explained. "He's obsessed with her, basically. Anyway, Jess was predictably surprised and angry and sent him on his way with a few harsh words, or that's what it sounds like from the message thread. Ken apologised to her repeatedly, and over the following days, Jess seemed to mellow towards him and wasn't quite so fiery. I don't think she ever forgave him, though, because, from that day onwards, she was, by degrees, rude, insulting and just plain unkind towards him."

"Understandable," Jon remarked, as he absorbed this latest raft of information. With proof that Ken was both utterly obsessed with Jess, and that he knew where she lived, he'd suddenly shot to the top of the suspect list, as far as he was concerned.

"Absolutely," Kate agreed.

"I'd have done the same if I was Jess," Rachel added.

"He deserved it," Dion said. "And, to his credit, he's taken it. He's never complained and never asked her to stop. He has also been messaging her since her murder, asking where she is."

"Well, we'll be able to bring him up to date on that today," Jon said. "I want to speak to him as soon as possible."

"So, Jess must never have told her boyfriend about Ken's visit," Kate said.

"That seems to be the case," Dion replied. "I found messages from her shortly after Ken's visit, telling him that she'd tell her boyfriend about his visit if he wasn't careful and would send him round."

"Again, under the circumstances..." Jon said and shrugged.

"I agree," Dion said.

"And what about Ozzy?"

"That one seemed to play out more or less how Conrad said it did. Whereas Ken was never abusive, Ozzy was. He sounds like a real piece of work, to be honest, based on the vitriol in his messages to her."

"These keyboard warriors usually turn out to be frustrated teens," Rachel said, offering her insight.

"Sometimes, but not always," Jon added. "So he joined up, started messaging Jess, and then flipped, becoming abusive?"

"Basically," Dion confirmed. "He joined as an apparently normal fan, bought a few things from her, but I think he wanted more than she was willing to give, and when there were some delays in her replies, it infuriated him. He started sending abusive messages, threatening her in various ways, before she banned him. Later, he re-joined with new details, but it soon descended into abuse again. She told him to keep away, as she'd just ban him again, but he kept doing it. He'd create a new email and use that to create a new account and sign up. He'd also use a VPN to hide his identity, but it always ended in the same way. It's as if he couldn't restrain himself."

"You said he ordered a few things from Jess. Does that mean we have an address?"

"We have addresses for both of them," Dion confirmed. "Ken's checks out, and according to our records, he does indeed live at the address he gave Jess. Ozzy however, is another story. I've done a load of digging, but the address he gave does not belong to him, and he's not showing up in my searches, which could mean he's been using a fake name online or something. Or maybe he just doesn't have a permanent address or own property. It might be worth checking out the address he gave Jess, though. Could be a friend or something?"

"Could have been using a friend as a free PO Box," Jon guessed. It was a clever tactic and showed foresight. It suggested that Ozzy knew what he'd end up doing, and had planned ahead.

"That was my thought. Either that, or he just used a random address and didn't care where she sent the stuff he bought off her."

Jon shrugged. "We'll know soon enough. That's great work, Dion. Thank you."

"It's not all, either," Dion replied. "We've been looking into Jess's final movements too."

"And what do you have?"

"Not much yet," Dion admitted. "The only thing of significance that stands out is a trip to a nightclub a few nights before her death. We're going through street cams and trying to get the nightclub footage too. As soon as we have anything of interest, we'll let you know."

"She could have met her killer at that club," Kate reasoned. "Maybe that's where she pissed him off?"

"That's possible." Jon turned back to Dion. "I want to know everyone she spoke to that night."

"I'll do my best," Dion replied.

"That's all I ask," Jon said, and looked around the table. "What else?"

"I've been talking to some of Cathy's friends," Kate said, referring to Jess's missing mother. "One in particular, actually, who seemed to know more about the night Cathy went missing than the others. She confirms that Cathy was scared of Mickey, which is why she left him. He was apparently violent and prone to coming in drunk and causing problems. Smashing things. Being violent. He was just a nightmare, basically."

"Why did she sneak out?" Rachel asked.

"According to this friend, it was because Mickey was very controlling and said he'd never let her go. He said that he'd hunt her down and drag her back. So she planned to leave in the dead of night and abscond. She only gave certain details to this one friend, who'd been a mate of hers since school. According to them, Cathy was supposed to call once she'd made it to safety."

"Let me guess," Jon cut in. "She didn't call?"

"No, she didn't," Kate confirmed. "But she did text once, literally to say she was safe, but that was the last anyone heard from her."

"I'm willing to bet she wasn't safe," Jon remarked, seeing where Kate was going with this. "And I'd also be willing to bet that she wasn't the one to send that text."

Kate shrugged. "Your guess is as good as mine, guv."

"Why didn't she just leave during the day, when Mickey was at work or something?" Dion asked.

"Again, according to this friend, it was because she'd have been seen, and she was terrified that Mickey had people in her street watching the house and her. Mickey was well thought of and liked by the local crooks, apparently, and had something of a following."

"That's messed up," Dion commented.

"Aye," Jon agreed. "So it looks like we have either one psycho, who killed Jess and her mother, or two, and a very unlucky family."

"It's like buses," Dion said.

"You what?"

"Well, I just mean that you don't get any for ages, and then two turn up at once. You know?"

The table was silent.

Jon fixed Dion with a look, and after what felt like an eternity, finally found some words. "Yeah, just like buses... So anyway, back in the sane world, Kate, any news back from the officer we put on Mickey? Has he done anything of note?"

"Nothing yet, guv."

"Alright, well keep him there and let's see how that pans out, but in the meantime, we need to chase up these fans of Jess. Kate, you and I will head over to Ken's and have a nice friendly chat, see what he's got to say for himself. Meanwhile, Rachel, can you check out that address for Ozzy, see who lives there. Take someone with you, if you can."

"Will do, guv," Rachel replied.

"Perfect, let's get to it. And Dion?"

"Yes, boss?"

"Have a word with yourself."

15

Jon turned into the arse end of Redhill. However, he'd probably have changed its name to Redhell, if he'd had his way. He navigated his way through the council estates, dodging delinquent children who should have been at school as they walked around in their best hoodies, looking for all the world like little terrorists.

Jon just rolled his eyes as they passed the suspicious-looking groups peering in at him and Kate. He felt confident that he could roll up on them, and providing he managed to detain them, he'd likely find something on them that he could book them for. Such was the nature of gang life in the urban areas these days.

"You think this is our man?" Kate asked, no doubt referring to Ken.

"Don't know. But if what Dion said was true, and he did turn up on her doorstep, then that makes me very suspicious. Doesn't it you?"

"Oh yeah, for sure. But I'm withholding judgement until I meet the man."

"Very wise," Jon said. "He seems keen on Jess, though."

"He does," Kate replied, and pulled out her phone. "I've got the transcript of their texts the night she was murdered, and he messaged her just before she was killed saying he was thinking of her."

"You mean, like the killer was, who was probably hiding in her house at that point."

"That's exactly what I mean."

"Sounds like you've condemned him more than I have."

"I just think it's a bit sketch, that's all."

"There you go again, being all down with the kids. Next thing, you'll be releasing your rap album."

"I don't think I'm quite there yet," Kate said. "Besides, I think the brass might have an issue with me moonlighting."

"I'd buy it."

"You'd damn well better, homeboy."

Jon smirked. "Stop, just stop. It sounds so wrong coming out of your mouth."

Kate laughed as Jon pulled into a cul-de-sac and drew up to the kerb outside a small new-build terrace house. The whole road didn't look more than maybe ten years old, but it had suffered in the short years of its existence, with junk in several of the yards and replaced doors and windows looking very conspicuous.

There was a curious mix of cars on the road, from old bangers, to what looked like some kind of hot-hatchback with a body kit and flame stickers along the sides. It didn't look like a road that he would relish living on, that was for sure.

"Which one is he in?"

"That one," Jon said, pointing to the closest property, with its overgrown lawn and tired looking frontage. Ken had clearly never done a moment's work on the house.

"Nice," Kate said sarcastically.

"Let's go and make his day, shall we?" Jon got out and waited for Kate to reach him before crossing the short distance to Ken's front door. Jon pressed the doorbell and knocked before getting his warrant card ready.

The door opened, revealing a short, overweight, forty-year-old man with thinning dark hair struggling to conceal a growing bald patch, glasses, and a dodgy looking moustache. He wore baggy jeans and a t-shirt with a Batman logo on it.

"Hello?"

"Are you Ken Wyndam?"

"Yes."

Jon held up his warrant card. "Can we have a word?"

The man, who matched the photo they'd already seen, looked shocked. His face fell on seeing the warrant card as his eyes flicked back and forth between him and Kate. "Uh, what's going on? What's the problem?"

"Hopefully, nothing. But we need to have a chat. Can we come in?"

"Um." Ken glanced into his house and then back. "I, err... I mean, if you really want to... Don't you need a warrant for this?"

"Only if you don't invite us in," Jon replied, wondering what the issue was. "Have you got something in there you don't want us seeing?"

"Aaah, no. I mean, I was just in the middle of something, but... Ok, you can come in." Ken waved them forward and backed off. "Close the door."

Jon watched him hustle ahead of them and close a door off the hallway before guiding them right, into the front room.

The house stank. There was a stale, musty smell of someone who didn't air his place out or clean, and it seemed to pervade the whole environment. Jon glanced at the door Ken had just closed, wondering what might be behind it, before following Ken into his front room. Taking one look at the sofas, Jon discounted the idea of sitting down and remained standing in the half-light. The front curtains were almost closed, dropping much of the room into shadow, and in the shaft of light that sliced into the room, he could see the dust and other particulates as they danced through the air.

He almost coughed on seeing them.

"So, um, what seems to be the problem?" Ken asked, looking very uncomfortable as he shuffled from one foot to the other.

"We wanted to talk to you about Jessica Thornton," Jon began. "Or Jess_xxx as you might know her, on HoundPic."

Again, Ken's face dropped. "Oh. Oh shit. Look, it was a mistake. It was a moment of insanity, okay? I didn't mean to... I was just... I just wanted to see her, okay? I didn't think I'd scare her. That was the last thing I wanted to do. I didn't hurt her, I promise. I just had some gifts and wanted to say hi. I'm a fan. That's all. Oh, shit. Oh crap. Did she report me to you? Is that it? Oh god. I'm... I don't..." He clutched his chest and started to breathe heavily. "I need to sit down."

Kate was beside him instantly, guiding him into the closest seat. "It's okay, Ken. We just want to ask you some questions, that's all. Just calm down."

"But I didn't do anything. I knew I shouldn't have done it. Did she report me? Is that it? I'll stop messaging her if you want. That's fine. She doesn't need to see me ever again."

"Ken, please, calm down," Kate said.

"Okay, okay. Calm. Okay."

"We have some bad news about Jess, though, I'm afraid," Kate went on.

Ken seemed to stiffen and looked over into Kate's eyes where she crouched beside him. "Why? What? What's going on?"

"I'm sorry but, Jess is dead. She was murdered yesterday morning."

Ken seemed frozen to the spot, and for several seconds just stared at her. His only movement was the occasional blink.

"Mr Wyndam?" Jon said after waiting for a few seconds.

He looked up, seeming to snap out of the shock. "Uh, yes?"

"Did you hear what my colleague just said?"

"Uh, yeah, but... What do you mean she's dead? How can she be dead? I don't understand."

"We found her yesterday morning. She'd been brutally murdered, and we're investigating her death."

"Holy shit. Are you sure? I mean, are you sure it's her? It could be someone else."

"I assure you, it's her," Kate replied.

"But, why me? Why are you speaking to me?"

"Because you were one of her keenest fans, and you once appeared uninvited on her doorstep," Jon said. "So you knew where she lived, and ever since then, it's clear that she's held a grudge against you."

"A grudge?"

"She's not all that friendly to you, is she?" Kate suggested.

"Well, I guess not. But, we chat... or did. She didn't stop talking to me."

"True," Kate answered. "But I've seen those messages. She wasn't exactly kind and caring, either."

"I... guess not," Ken said, still looking aghast.

"Will you be okay now?" Kate asked. "You've got your breathing under control again, right?"

"Yeah, I think so," Ken said.

Kate nodded and stood up. "I'm just going to have a look around if that's okay?"

"Yeah, yeah, of course." Ken waved her away as his eye's glazed over and he became lost in his own head. He was probably suffering from mild shock.

"Mr Wyndam, because of your previous interactions with Miss Thornton, we were very keen to talk to you and find out where you were the night before last."

"I was here."

The answer was quick and seemed instinctual, Jon noted. "And can anyone vouch for you and confirm this?"

"No, I... I live alone. So no. I don't go out much. Just to cash my dole check, you know. I'm on disability."

"Is that right?"

"I've got back and leg issues. I'm not a threat to her. I wouldn't hurt Jess or anyone. I couldn't. It's not in me. I... I like her. She was always kind, talking to me over messages and stuff. But, I suppose she won't be able to do that anymore."

Jon sighed quietly as he watched Ken talking. He seemed like a lonely, isolated man with few friends, who was just looking for some company, and it seemed like he'd found that in Jess. He'd found someone he could talk to and share some of his life with, even if it was just in a small way, through messages.

But was he a killer?

"Jon?" It was Kate.

"Yeah?"

"Come here."

Jon started to exit the room.

Ken's head jolted up as shock burst onto his face. "Oh, no. No, no no. Please. No."

He got up and followed, protesting the whole way, as Jon made his way out into the corridor, and turned to find Kate in the doorway of the room Ken had closed off.

"I think you should see this," Kate said.

"That's my private stuff, please," Ken continued to protest. "Please, just, don't..."

Jon stepped into the room as a new smell assaulted his senses. Like the rest of the house, it was a musty, icky stink that attached itself to the back of his throat and made him feel unwell. It wasn't helped by the scene he saw before him, either. The entire room had been plastered, from floor to ceiling, in printed off pictures of mostly naked women, and as he looked closer, he could see that Jess was amongst them. He'd printed off photos from her HoundPic feed and stuck them to the walls.

To his left, a large monitor on a computer desk displayed a paused video. Again, it was Jess, and she wasn't wearing much on the screen, either.

A moment later, Jon located the source of the stink when he saw the discarded, scrunched up tissues on the floor.

"I'm sorry," Ken spluttered from the hallway. "I didn't know. I wouldn't have... you know. Not if I'd known. Oh, Jesus. I know how this looks. It's not good."

Jon let out a long breath and looked back at Ken. The man was clearly obsessed—utterly obsessed—with Jess and several other young women too. They all looked like adults, though, which was a small silver lining.

Taking a step towards him, Jon planted his feet in the doorway. "Ken." The small man looked up. "Where were you the night before last?"

"I've told you. Here. I was here, alone. I don't know what you want me to do. How can I prove it to you? I didn't kill her. I couldn't. Christ, I get squeamish with needles and when I see blood. I couldn't kill someone. I don't have it in me to do that, and certainly not Jess. I... I love her... And I know that sounds stupid when you look at this room, but I do. She's beautiful. She's perfect. I know she hated me for what I did, I know I made a mistake and ruined any chance I had of being close to her, but I didn't care. I didn't care if she was mean to me. I deserved it..." He took a breath and sobbed. "I deserved it."

Jon met Kate's eyes as she gave him a look. He shrugged.

"It's okay, Mr Wyndam," she said, her voice soft and caring. "That's all fine. But I'd like to ask you to stay in the area, please, for the next few days, and we'll be in touch, okay?" Kate handed him her business card.

"Okay, of course." He sniffed. "I can do that. No problem."

"Thank you."

"Thanks, Mr Wyndam," Jon said. "We'll see ourselves out."

Outside, they got back into the car and sat for a moment.

"Well, that was... interesting," Jon remarked, as images of Wyndam's pleasure room, filled his mind's eye. "No matter what I see, doing this job, there's always something new just around the corner."

"He's just a lonely man," Kate said. "Harmless."

"It sounds like you pity him."

"Yeah, well, I guess I do. I've met others like him, before. They're plenty of them in the photography community, actually. Older men, usually single, who book shoots with models. Sure, they get to hang out with a pretty young woman who's usually not wearing much, and there's the creative aspect to it, too, but a huge proportion of them do it for the company. They're lonely, and they enjoy hanging out with these models. They mean no harm, and they're no danger to anyone."

"Yeah, I guess," Jon conceded, having come to a similar conclusion as well.

"Do you think he killed Jess? Is he our guy?"

"Right now, no," Jon answered. "But I've been wrong before."

"Yeah, me too. But I agree. He doesn't seem the type."

"No, he doesn't."

16

"Wow, that's a big building," Ellie said peering up through the front windscreen as they turned off the City of London road and pulled into the underground parking garage.

Nathan guided the car between the pillars of concrete and parked cars, making his way towards the police vehicles a short distance inside, beside an area that was fenced off, and sported an electronic gate.

"I didn't know we covered such a huge area," Ellie remarked.

It had been nearly a two hour car ride up into the very heart of London, fighting through traffic as the commuters made their way to work. But finally, they'd made it.

"Yeah, our remit with the National Crime Agency means we don't have a set territory or borders. The SIU can go anywhere across the country if need be. We're focused on Surrey and the Home Counties, as that's where we're based, but that's the only reason."

"Cool."

"We've not really travelled that far yet, though, for a case. This will be our first time up into the city," Nathan said, finding it curious that they had been focused on Surrey for so long.

"The SIU," Ellie replied, "it's kind of like the Flying Squad then, right?"

"Yeah, a similar kind of remit, but focused on murderers rather than robbers. We have more flexibility than a typical murder team because we deal with more specialised cases."

"The clue's in the name, I suppose. SIU. Special Investigations Unit."

"You're getting it. We'll make a detective out of you yet, Mizaki."

She patted her chest, mimicking a fluttering heart. "Oh, be still my beating heart."

"Sarcasm, too. Perfect, you'll fit right in."

"I noticed."

Nathan pulled the car into a vacant space, and the pair of them climbed out into the cool still air of the car park, lit by patches of artificial light in whites, tungsten, and the flashing blue of the Met police car that was close by. An officer was standing by the entrance to the car park. Nathan approached, revealing his warrant card, and the officer waved him in.

Nearby, a woman with long dark hair, wearing a long coat and business suit waited, talking to another officer. She saw Nathan approaching and moved closer to greet them.

She offered her hand. "DI Kristal Powers, with the MET. I take it you're DI Nathan Halliwell?"

"Correct, nice to meet you, Powers, and this is DC Ellie Mizaki."

They shook hands and swapped greetings.

"Was this your case?" Nathan said, feeling bad about sweeping in and taking the case away from her.

"It was," Powers answered. "But I'm busy enough as it is, so you can take this one off my hands with pleasure."

"The pleasure's all mine, I'm sure. I didn't want you to feel like I'm invading your territory."

"Not at all. Invade away, please," she replied, and then gave him a sideways look. "That sounds so wrong."

Nathan grinned.

"You'd fit right in at our station," Ellie commented.

"Ain't that the truth," Nathan added. "So, what have you got for us?"

"Well, before we head upstairs, I thought I'd meet you down here because there are a few things you should know before we move onto the main event."

"Of course, go ahead," Nathan replied.

"This is the VIP parking area where the building's wealthier residents park their cars," Kristal explained. Nathan eyed the sleek supercars, and high spec saloons on display, including a certain bright green Lamborghini that he'd seen before.

"I recognise that one."

"That's Grey Davison's, or one of his anyway. But that's not the reason I wanted to meet you. It's because the CCTV for this floor of the garage was taken offline, shortly before Grey was killed. Whoever did it was a professional, and we have no footage of anyone coming or going through here. Same for the corridors on the floor of his apartment."

"This was well planned," Nathan mused.

"Very well planned. We also think that one of the security guards was replaced with an imposter, who'd let certain people up the elevator."

"Did anyone see Grey or anyone else come through here?"

Powers smiled. "We do have one witness, yes," she said and directed Nathan and Ellie over towards a young man wearing what Nathan guessed was the building's uniform. "This is Stefan. He looks after the cars in this section of the parking garage, helps with luggage, that kind of thing. He saw Grey arrive."

Nathan gave the shaken young man a look. "You saw him?"

"Yes, sir." His voice sounded a little cracked and wobbly.

"Was there anything unusual about him?"

"No, nothing. He seemed fine," Stefan replied.

"You're sure?"

"Yeah. I've known him for ages now. I'd know if something was wrong. We talked briefly, and he tipped me for the work. But that's all. He often brings young women back with him, but he was alone tonight."

"Is that unusual?"

"No. He's alone maybe half the time, or a little more."

"What work did you do for him?"

"I put the cover on his car… which the police took off again."

Nathan glanced back at the green supercar and noticed the grey fitted cover that was still covering the front part of the vehicle. "Okay. Was there anything else unusual about tonight? Anything at all?"

Stefan glanced at DI Powers, who nodded at him, encouraging him. "There was one thing. The guard on the lift, I'd not seen him before today, and he didn't seem to know much about what he was supposed to do. Also, he disappeared shortly after Grey returned home, and I've not seen him since."

Nathan turned to DI Powers and raised an eyebrow.

"We looked into it," she said. "The usual guard didn't come into work today, and despite our calls, we couldn't raise him. So we sent someone round, and he found the guard restrained in his flat. Apparently, he was attacked by a masked gang who beat him, tied him up and stole his clothing. The mystery man appeared for work in the employee's place and bluffed his way through to here. We also think there might be someone else on the inside who helped him. We're looking into that."

"Were there any other new visitors who came through here around the same time as Grey?" Ellie asked Stefan.

"Urr, no, I don't think so."

"Okay, thanks."

"Shall we head up?" Inspector Powers led them into the lift, past a new guard, and punched the button for the upper floors.

Nathan took a closer look at the panel of buttons for the building's various floors. "Is this a dedicated way up?"

"It is," she explained. "It goes from the exclusive parking to all floors, but on the more public floors, you exit into a locked lobby before exiting into the building proper, using a key that only certain residents have."

"Are there other ways up to the floor where Grey lived?"

"Absolutely, there has to be for safety reasons," Powers answered. "So, am I right in thinking you know who did this? Care to let me in on the secret?"

"Lichwood was murdered by a man called Terry Sims. He's a former employee of Lichwood's, and the group Elden belonged to. He's a thug and a killer who took the fall for his boss, only for him to get locked up anyway. Terry seems to be taking revenge on these former employers following his recent escape from prison."

"And he came all the way up into town for this one?"

"Looks that way."

"He sounds like a piece of work."

"You have no idea," Nathan replied, as his mind flashed back to his previous encounters with Terry. He banished those thoughts as quickly as he could. It wasn't something he relished remembering, but this case was dredging up some disturbing memories. He'd not slept terribly well last night as images from Terry's invasion of his home several years ago haunted his dreams, causing him to wake up in the dead of night, drenched in sweat, convinced that the killer was in his house again, back to finish the job.

The lift doors opened, and DI Powers led them out in the corridor where Nathan spotted more police officers and their equipment behind police tape that sectioned off an area of the hallway. Powers led them into a huge, luxury penthouse apartment with clean, modern décor that had a distinct masculine quality to it. This was a bachelor pad, and the view over London was spectacular.

"This is Grey Davison's place," Powers announced. "One of several, I might add."

"The man's rich," Nathan muttered. "I'd be shocked if he only had one house or apartment."

"Come over here, I want to show you what brought us to you." Powers led them over to a desk at one end of a huge, open-plan corner living area, where Grey had a small office set-up, complete with desk and chair. A man was sitting there, going through a laptop and making notes. He looked up as Powers approached.

"Bring up the message," she said to him.

In a couple of clicks, a messaging system Nathan didn't recognise appeared with a single post. The sender was labelled as Elden Lichwood, but the message contents made it clear that Elden was dead, and the message came from his lawyers. "Once we linked it to Mr Lichwood, our systems linked it back to you guys, and that was that. Bingo-bango."

"I see, and it looks like they were trying to warn Grey."

"Unsuccessfully."

"Can you get to any other messages?" Nathan directed his question to both DI Powers, and the officer at the laptop.

"Nothing yet, no, and there are some complex security features in place on this device. We're lucky we got this."

"How did you get it?" Ellie asked, curious.

"He had his screen set to never turn off and not require a login once you exit the screensaver. Rookie mistake."

"The constant logging in probably annoyed him," Ellie said. "I get it. I hate that we have to do that back at the office."

"Me too," Nathan agreed.

"Well, we daren't move it or turn it off or anything, not until we have what we need," Powers explained.

"Alright, I'll leave that to you, then," Nathan said. "And Grey himself?"

"He's in the bedroom."

She led them back across the room, into another hallway and finally into a bedroom. Grey lay on his back, on the bed, his head towards them, hanging over the end of the bed. He was tied up, his wrists and ankles attached to the four bedposts, immobilising him. The man's face was fixed in a rictus of pain, his eyes open and vacant as blood dried around the single bullet wound in his head. He also sported several purple bruises on his face and a few more on his torso.

Nathan took a moment to scan around the room and quickly spotted the same dragon logo spray-painted on the wall.

"Just like Lichwood," Ellie said.

"Apart from the bruising," Nathan added. "Looks like he was beaten up."

"That was my guess too," Powers said. "He wasn't badly beaten, but it must have hurt, and he had no way to protect himself."

"Brutal," Ellie commented as she took notes.

"So, Lichwood was executed too?" Powers asked.

"He was," Nathan confirmed. "But without the torture, which makes me wonder… why?"

"No idea," Powers answered. "But I wish you well with it because it's not my problem anymore. Good luck."

"Thanks," Nathan replied.

"Catch you later." And with that, DI Kristal Powers walked out.

Nathan watched her go and then turned back to Ellie. "Another fine mess."

"Mmm," she answered, probably missing the admittedly ancient reference.

17

Finally making her way into Sutton, Rachel navigated through the suburban backstreets at the northern end of town before she found the street she was looking for. It was nothing special or unusual and featured a mix of council housing and private property. She'd been in much worse neighbourhoods over the years of hunting for criminals as part of her job.

Typically they were found in the less wealthy areas of any given town or city. It was something of a cliché by this point, but it was also, unfortunately, just a fact of life. There simply weren't the opportunities for poorer kids compared to those with more resources. And with the cost of living going up, she couldn't help but wonder what would happen to the next generation as they became teenagers and then young adults.

Poverty created crime, and it was evident there would be a lot more of the former in the coming years and decades, which would result in more of the later down the road.

Crawling along in second gear, Rachel soon picked out number fourteen and found a nearby place where she could park up.

She sighed as she glanced at the empty seat beside her, annoyed that she wasn't able to find someone to go with her on this hopefully routine house call. Dion was busy managing a team of researchers, and doing his own investigating. He'd offered to go with her, but she'd refused. He was needed back at the station to help progress the case. Besides, she was more than capable of protecting herself.

Steeling her nerves for what she was about to walk into, she climbed out and walked towards the house.

It was a modest semi-detached house with nothing really very outstanding about it. The building blended into the others around it, as one of hundreds of similar homes in this area. A few quick glances at the windows failed to reveal if anyone was inside before she rang the doorbell and waited.

"Hello?"

Rachel turned to see a man on the path outside the house, holding a bag of shopping in one hand and a new set of toilet rolls in the other.

"Can I help you?" he asked and approached the same door Rachel was standing before.

"Hello, yes. Do you live here?"

"Yeah, this is my home. Who are you?"

Satisfied she was talking to the right person, she showed her warrant card. "I'm Detective Rachel Arthur, with the Surrey Police, and I'd like to ask you a few questions, if I may?"

"Urr, yeah, sure. Anything I should be worried about?"

"Hopefully not. Do you live with anyone? Is anyone else in the house?"

"No, I live alone."

Rachel felt herself relax a little at his answer, pleased that she wasn't going to be walking into a house with more people in it. This also told her a little about what she wanted to know in what seemed like an innocuous question.

Ozzy didn't live here, or didn't any more at the very least. Unless this was Ozzy? She decided to find out. "What's your name?"

"James," he replied. "James Croft."

"Nice to meet you James," she replied, her confidence growing. "Shall we head inside?"

"Okay." James placed his shopping on his doormat, unlocked his front door, and led her into the hallway of his house, looking a little nervous. She followed him through to the kitchen, where a dog got up to greet them, and came sniffing round her.

"Don't worry, he's a big softy."

She scratched behind the dog's ears as James placed his bags on the countertop before turning and leaning on it. "So, what can I do for you?"

"Hopefully you can help me with my enquiries. But before I get into that, can I see some kind of ID? Something with your name on it? A driver's licence maybe?" She just wanted to be sure who she was talking to.

"Of course, hold on." James pulled a card out of his wallet, and passed it to her.

Rachel glanced over the driver's licence, noting that the name and face matched the man before her, and handed it back. "Thanks. But I'm actually looking for someone who goes by the name Ozzy. I'm not sure if Ozzy is their real name or just an online name, but we were hoping you might be able to help, because he once gave this address as a place he could be reached."

"Oh. Ozzy."

"Yeah. Do you know him?"

"Ozzy Gardener? Yeah, I know him. Why, what's he done now?"

"I can't go into details, but how do you know him?"

"He's a mate, you know? I knew him in school, and we've hung about a bit. Not so much recently, though."

"How come?"

James screwed his face up as if he wasn't sure he should tell her before he finally relented. "He's turned into a bit of a dick, really. He never lived here, though."

"Did you take any post for him? It might be a while ago. Over a year?"

"Oh, shit, yeah. I did. Aaah, okay. Yeah, he had a couple of things sent to me. I didn't know why, really. I think he said something about not wanting his housemates getting them or something. I can't remember. But yes, he did use me as a post box."

"Okay, well, we'd very much like to speak to him. Do you know where I can find him?"

"I think so. I don't think he's moved. He's in Epsom." James gave her Ozzy's house number and street name, and Rachel noted it down. "Are you sure you want to go and visit him?"

Frowning, Rachel looked up. "We need to follow up on him, so yeah, we will."

"You wanna be careful. He can be a bit of a handful."

"Is that right? Well, we'll play nice," Rachel assured him. "Don't worry."

James shrugged. "Alright, whatever."

A short time later, Rachel was back in her car, heading South West, back towards Epsom and the address that James had given her.

"You're heading there now?" Jon asked over the phone speaker that she'd attached to the dash mount.

"It's on my way, so why not?"

"Because of what you just told me," Jon said, sounding a little stressed. "His mate said he can be a handful."

"And I've got my taser, pepper spray, and baton with me, Jon. I'll be fine, and if he tries anything, he's going to get electrocuted, a face full of mace, and a bump on the head."

"Rachel, I think you should hold off. Just wait until someone can get there and back you up."

"I'm not waiting forever," Rachel answered, keen to bring the man in and maybe help close the case.

"We'll turn around and meet you, alright? Hang tight until then."

"Yeah, alright," Rachel answered.

"Good."

The phone call ended.

Rachel grimaced at Jon's comments but knew he was only looking out for her. It was good police practice to never go into a situation like this alone. Waiting for back up was always the right thing to do, but it was also not always possible or practical. With police numbers this low, they were frankly short-staffed. She was aware of countless times when she'd been forced to do something alone when she strictly shouldn't, and she wasn't the only one.

That was just the nature and reality of policing right now, and it wasn't about to change any time soon.

Rachel pressed on, driving into the outskirts of Epsom and through to the estate that James had directed her to. Arriving on another typical suburban street, lined with simple boxy houses, she soon found the house she wanted and pulled up close by.

Switching the engine off, she settled back into her seat and proceeded to watch the house, wondering if she might catch sight of this mysterious Ozzy.

The minutes dragged on as she waited for Jon's car to turn into the street while residents walked by, giving her curious looks as they caught sight of her waiting. With the car stationary, it was all too easy for a passer-by to see some of the police equipment inside the unmarked vehicle, making her feel a little conspicuous.

As minutes passed with no sign of Jon or anyone else coming to assist, Rachel chewed on her lip as her impatience started to get the better of her. Jon might reprimand her if she went and knocked on that door before he got here. He wouldn't be pleased if she got herself into trouble.

Checking on the gear in the car, she grabbed the taser and felt its weight in her hand. Holding it made her feel just a little more confident and safe. These things could drop a man in a heartbeat and were crazily effective.

"Screw it," she blurted out and climbed out of the car, stuffing the taser into the back of her belt.

Crossing the road, she strode up to the front door and rang the bell.

18

"We'll turn around and meet you, alright?" Jon said. "Hang tight until then."

"Yeah, alright," Rachel answered on the other end of the line. She sounded annoyed, and impatient. Not a great combination. But, there was little he could do from here, and he decided to end the call, and trust her.

"Good." He ended the call, feeling flushed and stressed. "Right..." he started to say before he heard Kate talking and realised she was on a call too.

"And where is he headed?" she asked. Jon frowned. What was *this* fresh hell? "Right, got it. I'm on my way." She ended the call.

"On your way? Where?"

"I need to get to the Surrey Hills," Kate explained. "Mickey's on the move."

"Mickey?" Jon's mind raced with possibilities as he considered what this might mean. Maybe it was nothing? Maybe he was just popping to the shops to pick up some milk or something. "It might be nothing."

"No, I don't think so. This feels off, somehow. Dyson agrees."

"Dyson? You got the Cleaner to be our stakeout guy?"

Kate shrugged. "Yeah, why not. He was keen to help, so I put him on the rota. They've been followed Mickey around. He's been out a few times, looking stressed. But this looks different."

"Why?"

"Dyson followed him into the countryside, not too far from his home. He's stopped in a dirt car park surrounded by woodland and walked into it carrying a huge bag."

"And Dyson saw him doing this, did he?"

"I guess so," Kate replied.

"Fine. I need to get to Rachel, though," Jon said. "I have a bad feeling she's going to do something stupid, like knock on Ozzy's door."

"Then go, drop me at the station. I'll grab a car and do my thing, and you do yours."

Jon pulled a face, disliking spitting up. But Kate would be with Dyson, and Rachel couldn't confront Ozzy alone. They weren't far from the station. He could drop Kate off easily enough and be on his way in moments. It made sense.

"Alright, fine. But be careful."

"Babe," Kate said, her voice taking on a patronising tone. "I think I'll be fine. Besides, I'll have Dyson there with me, and we both know what a big strong man he is."

Jon smirked as he imagined Kate single-handedly arresting Mickey while Dyson looked on, agape. "Fair point."

"The woman is always right, remember."

"So you keep saying," Jon replied and flashed her a wry smile as they approached the station. Jon pulled into the front car park, and Kate jumped out.

"Now go and give Rachel that backup. I'll see you later."

"See ya," he replied, but Kate had already closed the door and was running towards the pool-car garage at the rear of the building. Jon watched her go for a second before slamming the car into first and exiting back onto the road as quick as he could. He had a way to go but knew he'd be slowed by the traffic on the B-roads he'd be driving through. He wasn't sure this situation called for him to set the siren going and blast through some red lights. But after five minutes of fighting through traffic, he'd had enough and flicked the switch.

Blue light and noise exploded around the car.

Was this overkill? Would he turn into the road and find Rachel sitting in her car, waiting for him after he'd run through several red lights?

There was only one way to be sure.

No longer constrained by the speed limit, Jon sped through the Surrey countryside, doing his best to keep to the faster A-roads. Before long, he'd navigated his way around the Leatherhead Bypass, bombed through Headley Common, and was heading north along the A217 towards Sutton, screaming past the other cars on the dual-carriageway. Moving into Sutton itself, he was forced to slow. As he approached the road where Rachel was hopefully waiting for him, he turned off the siren and lights just before turning in to find Rachel's car empty on the side of the street.

"Shit." Jumping out, he scanned the nearby houses and spotted the one he was interested in, number four, and jogged towards it. The front door was closed, and there was no sign of Rachel.

He glanced through the front window and saw nothing.

Where was she? Had she done exactly what he'd asked her not to and knocked on Ozzy's door? He'd need to have a word with her later if she had, but he also understood the frustration of being forced to wait until backup arrived. It always felt like an age.

Jon knocked on the door as loud as he dared and waited. He thought of just kicking it in, but he didn't know if that was necessary yet and forced himself to remain calm. He took a long breath as he listened, straining to hear what might be going on inside.

A moment later, he thought he heard something. It sounded somewhat human, but muffled and unclear. He leant in towards the door, hoping to hear it again, but didn't. With a frown, he moved to the front window and peered inside again. Still nothing.

He heard a thud and then several distinct muffled cries or calls. The hairs on the back of Jon's neck stood on end. He needed to get in there. He tried the handle, but it was locked.

"Crap."

Taking a step back, Jon lifted his leg, and slammed his foot into the door. He aimed close to the handle, hoping to break the lock, and thanked whatever powers were watching over him that the door wasn't one of those modern U-PVC ones that took a battering ram to open.

Wood splintered on this third kick, and the door flew open with a bang.

Jon stormed inside.

A man in his twenties had hold of Rachel by the neck up against the wall. She clawed at his hand and gritted her teeth, her face desperate and scared.

The man, Ozzy presumably, glanced at Jon in shock. Ozzy dropped Rachel and charged at him. Jon was caught off guard as the man slammed into him, shoulder first. Sent reeling, Jon hit the door with a crunch which knocked the breath out of him. The man probably worked out, judging by the circumference of his arms.

"Fucking pigs," he muttered as he loomed closer and balled his fists.

Mentally preparing himself for a fight, Jon waited for the inevitable. "Ozzy, I'm arresting you for assaulting a police officer, wasting my bloody time, and ruining my day."

"You're funny," the man replied and lunged.

Jon tensed.

The man froze in his tracks and spasmed. An electrical clicking came from somewhere behind Ozzy. A moment later, the man dropped to the floor and trembled for a few seconds, before the clicking stopped, and he fell still.

Behind him, still sitting on the floor, Rachel held out her taser with two thin wires connecting it to the man's back. Rachel breathed heavily and looked like she was in a mild state of shock. He knew how she felt.

"Well," she said, looking at Jon. "Arrest him."

"That's the thanks I get, is it?" Jon got up, his back aching as he grabbed his cuffs from his belt. "Are you okay?"

"Oh, yeah. Never better. I can't get through a day without being strangled."

"What you and your husband get up to in your spare time, is none of my business. Glad to see you've not lost your sense of humour, though."

"Now *that* I can't get through a day without."

Standing beside the twitching man, Jon pointed at him. "I take it this is Ozzy?"

"Yeah, I think so." Rachel started to get to her feet also.

"Awesome." Jon cuffed him without resistance as the man moaned and groaned on his hall floor. "Ozzy, can you hear me?"

"Piss off," he grunted.

"I'll take that as a yes," Jon said, and began reciting the police caution, placing the man under arrest. "You and I need to have a chat. About your internet habits."

"I'll looking forward to it," Ozzy replied. "Sounds fun."

"Oh, it will be," Jon replied and hauled the man to his feet. "You don't have a special room, too, do you?"

"A what?" Ozzy asked, bewildered.

"Nothing." Jon guided the man outside where a couple of neighbours were already standing outside their houses, looking on. "Nothing to see here," he called out.

Reaching his car, Jon guided the man inside and closed the door before looking back at Rachel. "Are you sure you're alright?"

"I'm fine, don't worry about me."

"It's worrying about you that saved your life."

Rachel shrugged. "I could have taken him."

Jon grunted. "We'll have a chat about this later."

"Can't wait."

19

Pulling out onto the road, Kate turned towards Leatherhead, and powered out of Horsley. On the dash, her phone navigated towards where Sergeant Louis Dyson would be waiting, allowing her to concentrate on getting through traffic as quickly as she could.

Moving out of the dog-leg turn through the village, she was soon making good time, and her mind began to process the events of the morning and their curious encounter with Ken Wyndam. She'd met some odd people in her time on the force, but she'd long ago concluded that most normal people were fairly law-abiding and didn't cause big problems. It was usually those who'd had an atypical life that came to the attention of the police. The underprivileged, the traumatised, or those whose life and choices led them down a certain path. But that was the way things were. Sometimes life would take a hard left at the lights, and if you weren't able to adjust quickly enough, well, then trouble lay ahead.

Mr Wyndam struck her as someone who'd struggled through life. If she had to guess, he was probably a socially awkward man who had trouble forming relationships with people, and over time, he became a loner and a recluse. The internet was probably a blessing to him, allowing him to socialise without actually going out and meeting people. He could also safely nurture his obsessions and fantasies about this or that girl on the net, maybe even message them and develop some kind of friendship with them, however flimsy that friendship might actually be in real life.

Did Jess really care that much about the people who paid her a monthly fee to see the explicit photos? Or did she only care about them while they continued to pay her money?

She no doubt appreciated the support and the money they pledged to her, but would she be as happy if they started turning up on her doorstep, asking for more?

Probably not, and in Ken's case, that exact scenario had played out for her.

She couldn't imagine the utter shock and abject horror that Jess had experienced once she realised that the faceless name on the computer screen was standing at her door,

Ken seemed to believe he had a deep emotional connection to her, that she was more than just a face on the internet. To him, she was a lover, a long-distance lover who showed him sexy pictures and videos, sent him personal items, and continued to hold a long and meaningful discussion with him.

Sure, most of Jess's fans were probably better adjusted than that and knew the difference between fantasy and reality, but there would always be those who didn't, and that was where the cracks appeared.

Seeing Ken's shrine to the girls he obsessed over had been a shock, but she'd also half expected something like it. Perhaps not to that extent, but it wasn't a total surprise. That room was creepy though, and gave off strong serial killer vibes as far as Kate was concerned. She'd seen similar rooms in the past used by some of the most twisted and evil people she'd ever met.

Ken didn't seem evil, though, just misguided and naive, but they couldn't discount him yet. That room and his obsession could—if push came to shove—turn ugly. Maybe it already had?

Would Ozzy be as bad as Ken had been? He certainly seemed to have a cruel streak, given his messages to Jess. She hoped Jon and Rachel were okay.

After having turned south, Kate had soon found herself in the Surrey Hills, around Ranmore, an area of natural beauty that she'd spent some enjoyable walks in on her days off. But these wild open spaces were also occasionally the perfect place for the less savoury elements of society to ply their trade, and as she turned into the car park, she wondered what it was that Mickey was up to in here.

She spotted Dyson standing beside his unmarked car, looking tired and quite different now he was in plain clothes.

She was so used to seeing him in his uniform, it was odd to see him in civies.

"Kate, good to see you," he said, walking towards her. "He's still in there. God only knows what he's doing."

"Hopefully nothing," Kate replied. "It's good to see you too, Dyson. You look good in that suit. Have you ever considered a detective role?"

"Nah, it's not for me. I'll leave that up to you guys. You're the brains of the department."

"Awww, so you do love me."

"Err... yeah..."

"Which way did he go?"

Dyson pointed off into the woods as Kate scanned the area and took in the environment. The car park was a small open area on the side of the road made from packed earth with a sprinkling of stones and gravel. Several other cars were parked up, and as they talked, Kate saw a woman walk back to her car with her dog.

"And which is Mickey's car?"

"That one," Dyson replied, pointing to one on the other side of the clearing.

Kate wandered over and peered in through the windows. She wasn't sure what she'd find, but it never hurt to check.

Dyson watched her while keeping an eye on the woods as she moved around the vehicle.

"Everything alright?" the woman called out, after putting her dog in the boot of her car.

"Fine, thank you," Kate held up her warrant card. "We're with the police."

"Oh, okay, sorry. Anything I should be concerned about?"

Straightening up, Kate wandered a little closer. "Did you by any chance see who drove this car in here a short time ago?"

"No, sorry. I've been out walking for the past hour."

"And did you see anything unusual while on that walk?"

"Not really, no. Why, what's going on?"

"Hopefully, nothing. Thanks for your help. Can I take your details?"

"Sure, no problem." The woman gave her name and contact details before getting into her car. Nearby, Dyson was taking photos of all the other car number plates with his phone.

"Just in case," Dyson explained once he'd finished. "What now?"

"Now we go hunting." Kate surveyed the woods. "Which way did you say he went?"

Dyson took a step back to get his bearings, before pointing confidently. "That way."

"Not up one of these pathways? He went up there, through the bushes and into the undergrowth?"

"That's the way he went," Dyson confirmed. "I watched him scramble through there as I pulled in."

"Alright." Kate nodded. "I just wanted to be sure."

"I'm sure."

"Let's go then." Kate strode to the edge of the car park and pushed through a thicket of bushes that snagged her clothing, scratching her through the fabric. After scrambling up a steep bank, she reached level ground again, but there was no easy way forward from here. Trees were everywhere. The ground was covered in grass, leaves and twigs, as well as the occasional fallen branch.

Dyson followed, grunting and complaining as he climbed. While she waited for him to join her, she scanned the scene ahead, checking for movement or any hint of where Mickey might be.

Wiping the mud from his hands, Dyson grimaced as he reached her. "Christ, I should have put my walking boots on."

"Think yourself lucky. Mine have more of a heel on than yours."

Dyson looked down. "They're not that bad. They're almost flat."

"Yeah, well... still. Some wellies would be useful right about now."

"Amen to that."

Kate continued to scan the forest. "What was he wearing? What colours?"

Dyson thought about her question for a moment. "A dark blue top, black trousers, and he was carrying a black bag.

"Okay, well, I can't see him. Let's spread out and head this way." She pointed off in the same direction they'd set off in, guessing that Mickey would have walked in something of a straight line from the car park.

They walked cautiously but steadily through the forest, over ten metres apart with Dyson on Kate's left. Keeping a lookout, she did her best to avoid snapping twigs or making too much noise. Pushing through bushes and branches and the leaves rustling underfoot made it impossible to be completely silent. But if they could spot Mickey at a distance, they might be able to sneak up and get the drop on him.

Several minutes later, Kate caught sight of some movement up ahead and stopped. A moment later, Dyson realised he was leaving her behind and paused too, looking back.

Someone was up ahead, and by the looks of things, it had to be Mickey. The outline and colours were right, but they were partially obscured by the surrounding foliage, and he kept crouching down or bending over.

She pointed ahead. Dyson looked and took a few steps sideways before he froze and nodded back to her. "I see him," he hissed, keeping his voice low. "It's him."

Kate put a finger to her lips and shushed him before she made a gesture with her hands that indicated they should flank him.

Dyson nodded back and set off.

Picking out her own route, looking for cover and clearer sections of ground, she set off, moving more cautiously than before, always keeping one eye on Mickey as he bobbed up and down, in and out of sight.

At one point, he stopped and wiped his brow with his sleeve before taking a breath. Kate ducked down and indicated that Dyson should do the same as Mickey looked around. But once he was engrossed in his work again, they pushed on, closing the gap on him.

With only a few metres to go, Kate kept her eyes fixed on Mickey, ready to run towards him should he suddenly make a bolt for it. She needed to get just a little closer and narrow that gap a touch more.

A twig snapped beneath her foot.

Kate glanced down in shock at her bad luck before quickly looking back up, right into Mickey's eyes. He appeared shocked, and for a moment, they were frozen in place, their eyes locked for what felt like a terrifyingly long time. What would he do? How would he react?

With a shout that was little more than a guttural, almost inhuman grunt, Mickey charged at her. He burst through the bushes between them, carrying something.

It was a large shovel with a dirty metal end, the green paint scratched off by heavy use. He raised it high above his head.

Kate surged back and away as fear gripped her. Her right foot caught on something. Foot twisted and unable to regain her balance she fell onto the ground.

"No, no, stop," she yelled, her hands outstretched in a futile effort to protect herself.

A dark blur flashed across her sight and hit Mickey. Dyson slammed into him, putting his entire weight behind it. The pair went tumbling into the tall grass.

Mickey yelled.

"Give it up," Dyson shouted.

"Get off me," Mickey spat.

Kate jumped to her feet and ran over as Mickey tried desperately to get an angle on his attacker and hit him with the shovel. Lunging forward, Kate reached for it. She got one hand to it as the blade caught her other one.

"Aaagh," she yelled.

Mickey tried to yank it from her. Kate went with it and threw her body at the tool, grasping it finally.

She ripped it from him and threw it away before turning back and grabbing him. He fought and wrestled, but he was already tired, and two against one was too much for him. Turning Mickey onto his front, they cuffed him and the fight finally went out of him. He gave up. Kate got to her feet, wrinkling her nose at the muddy stains on her trousers while holding her aching hand.

"I'll bill you for this, Mickey."

He spat at her from where he lay but missed by a good distance. The sentiment was clear, though.

"So what were you up to, back there?" Kate asked, catching her breath. Locating the spot where he'd been working, Kate wandered over, her legs suddenly like lead weights from the fatigue. She pushed through the bushes he'd been behind and peered down.

At the bottom of a shallow hole, Kate made out skeletal remains, the side of a skull partially uncovered, making it obvious they were human.

"Shit," Kate hissed. Was that Cathy, his missing wife? Was he digging her up?

"What have you got?" Dyson called out.

"We need to call this in," Kate replied. "There's a body buried here."

20

In his front room, Jon slumped into his chair and relaxed, letting his head fall back against the cushion as he let the stresses of the day drain out of him.

It was the end of a long, busy day, filled with interviews, car rides, and several revelations. His mind had been spinning, considering all the facts, wondering how they might fit together in the hope they would reveal Jess's killer. But right now, while there were plenty of suspects and people that Jon didn't trust, there was no clear murderer.

Not yet, at least.

Meeting the two stalkers had been an eye-opening experience. Both were infatuated with Jess to the point of obsession, but their methods and the way they displayed that affection had been quite different and bizarre.

Seeing Ken's special room was not something he'd forget any time soon.

Around him, Jon's house was as silent as the grave. Apart from the kitchen's mood lighting and the side lamp in the lounge, downstairs was in relative darkness.

But Jon didn't mind the subdued light. The station's oppressively bright lights were a little too much after a while, and he felt glad to get away, sit in the shadows and let himself relax.

It wasn't unusual for him to come home and take ten minutes, or even up to half an hour to unwind, letting his worries fall away before he went anywhere near his bed.

He'd learnt a long time ago that jumping straight into bed after a long day's work was usually a terrible way to get to sleep. It led to frustration, a lot of tossing and turning, and very little precious sleep.

After a few moments, Jon realised how dry his mouth felt and had a sudden need for a drink. With more effort than he would have liked, he got up and meandered through to the kitchen at the back of the house, where he poured himself some water. He drank it greedily, enjoying the cool liquid as it refreshed him and woke him up.

Replacing the glass back onto the countertop, he took a moment just to enjoy the feeling before he opened his eyes. When he did they fell on a shape in the darkness that he was briefly confused by, until it moved.

She took a step forward out of the shadows and smiled at him with those glossy, wet lips of hers, beneath dusky, alluring eyes.

"Ariadne." He wasn't totally surprised by her appearance. In fact, he felt more dismayed than anything else and sighed to himself. He didn't conceal his emotions.

"Pleased to see me, I see."

"Not really."

"Were you expecting me?"

"Kind of. I can't say I'm shocked that you've appeared on my doorstep again."

"It's nice to be appreciated," she purred and moved closer, her heels clicking on the kitchen tiles. "I like what you've done with the place."

Jon narrowed his eyes at the dark-haired woman's comment. She knew as well as he did that she'd installed the kitchen for him without him knowing about it until he returned home to find it there. It was another one of the many things she'd done that was no doubt carefully designed to place him in her debt. He didn't trust her at all and wasn't entirely sure what her motives and desires were towards him. But whatever they were, he didn't want any part of it. She was a deadly predator, a spider-woman, a black widow.

Opening the fridge, she scanned the contents and pulled out a bottle of wine. "Shall we?"

"Do I have a choice? Are you going to have a sniper shoot me if I refuse?" He still had vivid memories of the man who'd attacked him in his own home, only for the attacker to be shot through Jon's front window by someone outside, moments before Ariadne walked in and declared she'd saved his life, and he owed her a life debt, whatever that was.

He didn't care what it was, but he knew it wasn't good for him, and he needed to get rid of it. But that was easier said than done.

"Jon, dearest, you always have a choice."

"Do what you want," Jon replied and waved a dismissive hand at her.

"Thanks, sweetie. Now, where are the glasses," she mused as she rifled through his cupboards until she found a pair of wine glasses. "Not where I'd keep them, Jon, if you want my opinion."

"And you know I don't."

"Someone's salty tonight." She poured two glasses of wine as she spoke.

"I'm just done with your shit."

She placed the bottle back on the counter. "Really? Well, maybe you'll change your tone when I tell you why I'm visiting you. I'm here to help."

"You? Help me?" The prospect was positively terrifying.

"But of course. I'm nothing but a concerned, upstanding citizen, Jon. I want to help you bring in this dangerous killer, this thug, Terry, and I will do my best to help you."

"Terry?" Jon did his best to hide his surprise, but it wasn't easy. How much did she know about the case? "Well, I, for one, can't wait to hear this." He moved to a nearby stool. As he relaxed into it, he spotted Kate standing out of sight of

Ariadne on the lower steps of the staircase, listening in. She'd been upstairs using the bathroom when Ariadne had appeared. Jon did his best to style out his glance at Kate, hoping that Ariadne didn't notice.

To his relief, she seemed none the wiser.

"I have resources that you and the Surrey Police can't possibly hope to have," she went on. "I can do things that you, as an agent of the law, cannot. Which makes me a valuable asset. Surely you can see that, dearest."

"Alright then," Jon replied, bored of her posturing. He decided to call her bluff. "So tell me, what exactly *are* you doing to help me. I'd love to know."

"I know what Terry's doing—" she began.

"Whoop-di-doo," Jon cut in, hollering his fake joy to the ceiling. "Well then, we're saved. That was a complete mystery to us."

Ariadne narrowed her eyes, betraying her annoyance. "I could grow to dislike you, Jon. You do realise that."

"I live in hope." He shrugged, not too bothered by the implied threat.

After another long moment, she smiled suddenly and laughed. "Who am I kidding? How could I not like you, Jon? You're just too much fun."

"I'm glad I amuse you."

"Always. So, as I was saying, before I was rudely interrupted, like you, I know what Terry is doing, but I have some interesting information for you that you don't know."

"Enlighten me."

Ariadne smiled. "With pleasure. Did you know there's a Miller on Terry's crew?"

"As in the Miller family?" Jon asked, referring to the well-known Miller crime family in the area, who Jon had run across a couple of times during his time down here.

"No, as in someone who makes bread," Ariadne snarked before rolling her eyes. "Of course, I mean those Millers. His name's Felix Miller, and I've taken the liberty of informing Irving." She was talking about the current elder of the family, who, it was believed, ran their various criminal enterprises.

"Have you?"

"Yes, indeed. It was a lovely, fruitful meeting. Although, he's not as charming as you, my dear." Beyond Ariadne, he saw Kate roll her eyes. "So, I think you might find Terry's crew is weakened by one, at least."

"I doubt that will stop him from continuing with his mission," Jon replied, unimpressed, despite the ballsy move of meeting with Irving. "Besides, why would Irving bring Felix back in? This could be a deal between Terry and the Millers, for all you know."

Ariadne smiled again. "Oh, Jon. You really need to do more research. I'm putting you to shame here. Terry is not a friend of the Miller family. Before he worked for the Abban, Grey and the others in the Black Hand group, he was an enforcer for a rival gang. The Millers hate Terry, so they won't be very pleased with Felix for being on his crew."

Was that true? He felt like an idiot for not knowing and wondered how she'd discovered all this information.

"Oh, I see," Jon answered, doing his best to keep his face neutral and not betray his true feelings on the matter. She had enough of an ego as it was.

She chuckled knowingly. "That's not all."

"There's more?" This time, he was genuinely interested.

"There's someone else on Terry's crew that I think you might be interested to know about. Someone that might change things for you, on this case of yours."

"Nathan's leading the Terry Sims case, not me," Jon replied, unable to stop himself correcting her. He was being petulant and immature, but her self assured smugness just seemed to bring out that side of him.

Ariadne smirked once he'd finished, in a way that made him doubt himself within a second of finishing his reply.

"I know that," she answered, the humour and lightness in her voice gone for a moment. "I meant your case. The Jessica case."

Her uncanny knowledge of what went on in their unit only served to reinforce an idea he'd come to after the unit's last major case, that there was a leak inside the SIU. Someone was working for Ariadne, and feeding her information, but who? And was she implying that she knew of a link between the Terry case and the murder of Jessica?

"Go on," he urged, doing his best to not seem too interested, and keep calm.

"Henry Thornton is on Terry's crew."

Jess's brother? "Are you sure?"

"Do you doubt me, John?"

He narrowed his eyes at her. He was inclined to believe her, given her knowledge of the case and his previous interactions with her, but was he supposed to just take her at her word? She wasn't exactly giving him much in the way of proof. "How do you know all this?"

"I have my sources, and that's all you need to know. But, you know what this means, don't you, Jon?"

He felt his stomach sink at her words and wondered where she was going with this. "I feel fairly sure that you're going to tell me, whether I want you to or not."

She grinned at him, but it was the smile of a predator moments before they bit you in two. It didn't carry any joy with it.

"It means your debt to me, is increased. But, in return, I've saved your life, and I'm helping you solve your case, and maybe save lives. Am I not merciful?"

Jon felt a little sick at the thought. Looking up, he noticed Kate had stepped silently out from her hiding place and was standing in the doorway to the hall. Ariadne would be able to see her if she turned around.

"Aren't you just."

"Jon, be serious for a moment. I will need this repaid at some point, you know? "

"Will you..." he kept his tone deadpan.

"I will, but all in due time. There's no rush," she answered, her eyes fixed on his as she spoke. "Hello, Kate." She smiled at Jon.

"Ariadne," Kate replied, her voice even.

She turned to Kate. "Watching over your man, are you?"

"No," Kate replied as she sauntered closer with slow, easy steps. "Just thinking about how I'm going to haul your arse out of here."

Ariadne clamped her mouth shut for a moment, possibly a little shocked by Kate's reply, before she seemed to pull herself together a little. "Well, let me save you the trouble."

"Oh, no, it's no trouble. I'd quite enjoy it."

"Well, I've said what I came here to say. I'll leave you two love birds alone, shall I?"

Kate was just a couple of metres away from Ariadne with her arms crossed, her eyes locked on the woman. She didn't answer, she just stared at her for a long moment, and Ariadne stared back. Suddenly, Kate lunged towards her but pulled back at the last moment. Ariadne jumped, and Kate smirked.

"Get out." Kate's voice was low and threatening.

"Cheap shot, Miss O'Connell," Ariadne said as she walked away, making for the front door. "I hope you're proud of yourself."

"Incredibly."

Ariadne's left eyebrow twitched almost imperceptibly and her lips pursed briefly before she turned and walked down the hall. The sound from her heels echoed as she went.

"We'll call if we ever want a new kitchen, yeah?" Kate called after her.

The front door slammed shut. She was gone.

Kate turned to Jon. "She's a piece of work."

"You're not kidding." Jon picked up the two untouched glasses of wine Ariadne had poured and handed one to Kate. "Cheers."

They clinked glasses.

"I think you need me to move in," Kate said as she sipped her drink, "if only to keep Ariadne at bay."

"Like a guard dog?"

"Careful, Pilgrim," Kate said, with a bob of her eyebrows.

There she goes again, Jon mused to himself, suggesting that they move in together, and again it's in the form of a joke. She'd probably deny it and say she was kidding, but Jon wasn't so sure. He had no idea how the female brain worked, but he felt sure that this was her cute little way of planting the seeds and gently ushering him down the path she wanted him to tread. The thing was, she probably had a point. If Kate lived here, Ariadne almost certainly wouldn't just show up like she had been doing.

It was a tempting thought, and he began to wonder if he should actually broach the subject with her again?

Would she agree? But also, more importantly, was it a good idea for him? It had been five long years since he'd lost his girlfriend to that killer, and she had been the last person he'd shared a house with.

Could he do it again with Kate?

"Let's go and sit down," Kate suggested. "I'm shattered."

They wandered through to the front room, where Kate closed the curtains before joining Jon on the sofa, sipping her wine.

"So, Henry Thornton?" Jon said. "Do you think Ariadne's telling the truth?"

"Do you?" Kate asked.

He briefly considered the question, but he already knew the answer. "Actually, I do. I doubt she'd make something like that up. But, we can bring Henry in tomorrow and see what he's got to say for himself."

"Are you planning on saying you were told by Ariadne?" Kate asked.

"No. Ariadne and what she's said here tonight stays off the record. I don't want any of that entered into the case. After everything that's happened with her, I have no desire to risk the case or my career by getting her involved."

"Fair enough. We can bring him in easily enough. We need to, actually, after Mickey today. He needs to know what happened with his dad and what happened to his mother."

"Yeah, he does," Jon agreed. "Did you speak to Mickey?"

"Not yet, his lawyer's taking his sweet time. It looks like tomorrow at this rate. But it's all fairly damning. He knew where his wife was buried and was digging her up."

"Agreed. I hope the jury agrees too."

Kate nodded. "We can but try. So what happened with Rachel and Ozzy? I heard she messed up."

"Aye. She only went and knocked on Ozzy's door all on her own. I've got no idea what she was thinking. Anyway, according to her, he let her in, she asked him some questions about Jess, and then he turned violent and attacked her."

"And you brought him in?"

"We did, yeah. I've had a chat with him already, but so far nothing. He's got an alibi for the night that Jess was killed, too. He was with a few friends that night, and they've all vouched for him. He's an idiot and clearly violent, but he didn't kill Jess. We'll get him for assaulting a police officer, though. So that's something."

"Damn, so it wasn't Ozzy."

"Nope. Which leaves, Ken, Henry, and Mickey, and we know which of them appears to be a murderer."

"Yeah, we do."

21

"Right," Jon said as they walked through Horsley Station the following morning. "I think we all need to have a chat. You, me, Nathan and Ellie. Let's get everyone on the same page with all this. What do you think?"

"Yeah, you're right," Kate agreed. "If Henry is on Terry's crew, these two cases might be more closely linked they we initially thought. We'll bring Henry in and have another chat."

"That's the plan, but I do wonder if that might trigger Terry, and force him to... I don't know, do something rash?"

"We're limiting his options," Kate agreed.

"He might also think we're onto him, putting pressure on him." Jon led Kate into the main floor and over to his office.

"Meaning he's likely to make a mistake," Kate agreed, "like Mickey did when he went to dig up Cathy."

"What on earth was he thinking doing that?" It was bizarre behaviour.

"Whatever he was thinking, It wasn't logical, that's for sure."

"Mmm," Jon mused. "Well, hopefully, we'll learn a little more today. Why don't you go and gather up Nathan and Ellie, and bring them over?"

Kate agreed and went to find the pair as Jon stepped into his office and went about his usual routine of setting up for the day ahead. Within moments, he'd logged in and started bringing up the details of the Jessica Thornton case, and the Terry Sims case.

Was it all just a crazy coincidence? There was a distinct possibility that the link between Jess's murder and Terry's rampage was nothing but a bit of synchronicity. They'd known of Henry's criminal record and his involvement in the area's gang culture, and if Terry was the hot ticket of the week, maybe it was just too tempting to pass up. Maybe that was all it was, and Jess's death had no further link to Terry and his crew than that. But Jon couldn't shake the feeling that Ariadne was onto something with this. Had they been looking in the wrong place for Jess's murderer this whole time?

Leaning back in his chair, he frowned, frustrated with the situation. He checked his messages. It seemed that Mickey had finally had a little chat with his lawyer and was ready to speak to them. About time too. This hunt for Jess's killer was dragging out for far too long, and he was starting to worry that the man would strike again if they didn't bring him in soon.

Checking his to-do list, he was reminded that he needed to talk to Rachel about her actions yesterday. She'd put herself in unnecessary danger and was lucky she'd survived.

He was quite aware of the terrible state of the police across the country and in their own constabulary. They were criminally understaffed and under-funded, leading to cuts in patrols and services that should never have been allowed to happen. It meant they were often forced to do things alone when they shouldn't, but this felt like a choice made out of impatience rather than necessity. He wouldn't be too hard on her, she was only trying to do the right thing, after all, but even so, he couldn't allow his team to throw themselves into the firing line whenever they felt like it.

Looking away from the screen, Jon wiped some crud from his eyes and yawned, cursing his overactive brain and the lack of sleep it had given him once again. Seeing Ariadne in his home last night had set his mind racing, especially when it came to this so-called debt that he apparently owed her.

He had no issues with owing anybody a favour, but the whole thing with Ariadne felt so manipulated. The man who'd attacked him on this doorstep several months ago had felt like a set-up. It was all far too convenient that Ariadne was there at just the right time to save him. He knew Kate felt the same about it, and he didn't blame her. The whole thing stank of a set-up, and he certainly wouldn't put it past Ariadne to hire someone to kill him and then save him at the last moment.

He just dreaded the day that Ariadne came calling, wanting him to repay her.

Movement beyond his office door caught his eye. Moments later, Kate led Nathan and Ellie into his office and closed the door behind them.

"Morning, Guv," Nathan said.

"Sir," Ellie added.

"Good morning, guys. How's things?"

"Alright," Nathan answered. "We're still dealing with the fallout from Grey's murder and doing our best to work with the Met to get all the info sent over. He was killed in a similar way to Elden, with a single gunshot to his head. The main difference was that he'd been tied down and beaten beforehand. Otherwise, it was all too familiar, right down to the graffiti on the wall."

"Definitely Terry again, then?"

"I would say so, even without any CCTV."

"Well, hopefully we can pressure him into making a mistake."

"How?"

"Because of some additional information I received last night, which might come in useful."

"Oh, like what?"

"Well..." Jon went to speak but held back on realising Ellie was in the room and was probably unaware of the full details of his history with Ariadne. "Actually, before I get onto that..." He turned to the junior detective. "Ellie, has Nathan mentioned Ariadne to you?"

"Briefly, yes. She's some kind of rich..."

"...bitch," Kate added.

"Err, I wasn't going to..." Ellie stammered.

"I know," Jon said, "but Kate is right, she's caused all kinds of problems for us over recent months, on several cases, and has been something of a thorn in my side."

"She took a personal interest in you, didn't she?"

"She did, although the reasons for that are still something of a mystery to me. But, she's appeared a few times since that first case where she acquired a lot of money. Always showing up and causing trouble. Anyway, she visited my house again last night. She just appeared in my kitchen like it was nothing, saying she had some information on our cases. She knew you were looking into Terry's case, and we were on Jess's."

"She knows entirely too much, that woman," Nathan griped.

"Absolutely, and I have some ideas about that, too. Anyway, she told me two things. She said there's a member of the Miller family on Terry's crew who shouldn't be there..."

"Why?" Nathan interrupted.

"Apparently, it's because Terry once used to run with a rival gang, so there's bad blood between them."

"Oh, he did. She's right," Nathan replied. "I did some research on him back when he led that house invasion of my place. He was running with a rival gang back then."

"So, you knew?"

"Yeah," Nathan confirmed. "But it wasn't very relevant to this investigation until now."

Jon nodded, agreeing. Nathan was right. It made little difference to know Terry didn't get along with the Millers, not until Ariadne's revelation that there was a Miller on his crew. Had they found that out, he felt sure they'd have looked into it and discovered that rivalry themselves.

"Fair point," Jon said. "But she also told us that one of the other members of Terry's crew was Jess's brother, Henry."

Nathan's eyes narrowed as he listened. "Oh. So the murdered girl's brother is helping Terry with his murder spree?"

"Kinda suspicious," Ellie said.

"It does raise questions regarding Henry if he's happy to go around helping someone assassinate people," Kate agreed. "Makes me wonder what else he's capable of."

"Like, killing his sister," Ellie added.

"A sister he doesn't have a great relationship with," Jon said. "It's all very suspect."

"Are you bringing Henry in then, on the strength of that information?" Nathan asked.

"Well, first off, I'm not having any mention of Ariadne in this case report," Jon said. "I'm not going down that path."

Nathan wrinkled his nose but nodded. "Fair enough. That's your call. You didn't need to tell us."

"Secondly, we need to bring Henry in anyway after finding Mickey digging up Henry's mother," Jon said. "At the very least, Henry deserves to know all about this, and we'll see how it all goes from there. See what he says once we put it to him that we know he's on Terry's crew."

"He'll just deny it," Nathan said.

Jon shrugged. "Maybe. You never know. But this does make me wonder if there's a bigger connection to the Terry Sims case. Did Terry or other members of his crew know about Henry's sister?"

"Yeah, maybe."

"We could do with finding out," Jon said. "What about Lester? Would he know?"

"He might. He said he wasn't friendly with Terry anymore, but I don't know how recent that was. So yeah, we could ask him what he knows."

"Okay, sounds good," Jon said. "Let's see how this thing with Henry goes first, though. We'll bring him in, removing another person off Terry's crew."

"You're going to make him desperate if he's lost Henry and this Miller guy," Nathan said.

"That's the plan," Jon confirmed.

"What do you think he'll do?" Kate asked.

"I don't know," Nathan answered. "If he thinks we're onto him, and that he might not finish his mission, I think he'll speed up."

"Let's hope he makes a mistake," Jon said. "Something we can use against him."

"Mistakes can cost lives," Kate said.

Jon sighed, fully aware of the risks they were taking. "I know." He sat back and glanced over at Nathan, who was staring into the middle distance with a troubled frown on his face. After a moment's silence, Jon leant forward. "Penny for your thoughts?"

Nathan refocused, returning the conversation. "I was just thinking about where this information came from and wondered how Ariadne got it."

"That's been troubling me too," Jon admitted.

"You said you had some thoughts on it?"

"Oh, I do, but you're not going to like them."

"Do we have a leak?" Nathan asked. "It's the obvious conclusion."

"It is, and it's something I've been pondering. But we don't have much time right now to worry about that. We need to bring these cases to a close."

"Alright," Nathan agreed. "So, what's the plan?"

"Kate and I will have a chat with Mickey again, and in the meantime, I need you and Ellie to bring Henry in."

22

"I hope to bloody hell he talks," Jon said as he and Kate made their way towards the interview rooms where Jess's father waited for them. He'd been in the cells overnight, waiting for his lawyer, who'd finally arrived early this morning and spoken with him. The wait was annoying, but Jon hoped that a night stewing in the cells might give Mickey time to think through his life choices and work to their advantage.

"I'll keep my fingers and toes crossed," Kate replied. "I can't see how he can refute this now, though. We caught him red-handed."

"I know, but he could easily come up with some crazy story about... I don't know... the true killer taunting him by telling him where they'd buried her or something."

"Alright, let's say he does that. Then why keep it to himself? It only makes him look guilty. Also, if he did love her and know where she was buried, why would he leave her in a shallow, unmarked grave? Why not give her the burial she deserves? And why head out there in the middle of an investigation?"

"I know, I know," Jon agreed. "It wouldn't make any sense. Doesn't mean he won't try it, though."

Kate sighed. "True. Depends how desperate he is to stay out of prison, I guess."

They soon made it into the corridor lined with interview rooms and entered the one Mickey was in. Sitting behind the table, his arms were folded and resting on it. His head bowed, staring at the pockmarked top. Like all the tables in the other rooms, this one had seen its share of abuse and carried the scars to prove it.

Mickey's lawyer was sitting beside him, his folder closed as he waited. Jon introduced himself and Kate before sitting down, preparing the DIR and setting it to record. Mickey didn't acknowledge them the whole time and just waited in silence, making Jon feel uneasy. But there was nothing for it but to plough on and see how this all panned out.

With everything set, Jon introduced everyone for the benefit of the Digital Interview Recorder, asking them to identify themselves when asked. Mickey complied but still didn't move.

"Right then, Mickey," Jon began. "I hope your night wasn't too uncomfortable."

He closed his eyes and then looked up, keeping his head bowed. "It was fine."

"Good, good. So, let's start with a nice easy one, shall we? What were you doing in the Ranmore woods yesterday when my colleague here found you?"

Mickey closed his eyes briefly again and took a long breath. "Okay, you don't need to try and drag it out of me, I'm going to talk. I'm going to tell you what I was doing, and... and who is buried out there. I'm going to be honest."

"Are you? Well, great. Then please, in your own time." Jon waved a hand towards him, indicating that the floor was his.

"Before I get into it, I just want to apologise to you," he said, looking at Kate. "When I saw you, out there. I panicked and didn't know what to do, so I lashed out. I hope you're okay."

Kate gave him the barest hint of a smile and then nodded once. "Thank you, but I'm fine."

It was an interesting way to start, Jon thought, and wondered if this wasn't some kind of ploy to try and bring him and Kate onside and sympathise with him.

"Good, I'm glad." Mickey nodded and took another few seconds to himself before he continued on. "You understand that... this is hard. It's been a long time since..." He took another deep breath. "Okay, you don't need to know that. It's what it looked like, and the remains are who you think it is."

"We're going to need a little more than that, Mickey."

"I know, I know. I'm... I'm building up to it."

Jon raised his hands. "Alright, in your own time."

"The body, the one I was digging up, that's Cathy, and yes, I was the one who put her there." He took another deep, ragged breath as his adrenaline pumped. "We'd not been getting along for months before it happened, you know. We just disagreed on so much. She didn't like what I did to bring money in, she didn't like how I treated Jess. I'm not even sure if she loved me at the end. Probably not."

"Did you love her?" Kate asked.

"I think so, looking back. But she annoyed the ever-loving fuck out of me, too. I wasn't in a good place, things were tough, and the fighting between us just got worse. I'm ashamed to say I got a little violent too. That was something I never thought I'd do, ever. But there were nights when the rage was just too much. I was a jealous man, and I thought she was seeing someone. I don't know if she was or not, and that doesn't excuse anything, but that was how I was at the time. Then I found out she was going to leave me. That was the worst part, I think. I just got so jealous. I believed she was *mine*. *My* wife. Not someone else's. She couldn't leave me. How dare she... Well... That's how I felt at the time. I was just in a horrible place, filled with rage and fury.

"Then I heard through a friend that she was going to leave me. He'd overheard his girlfriend talking to Cathy. When he found out, he couldn't not tell me, and that's how I found out. Days passed, and I noticed little things as she started to prepare to leave me. I saw money being moved, and a bag hidden in a wardrobe being packed over several days. And then the day came. So I laid awake, waiting until she made her move.

"I remember feeling her get up and out of bed. She grabbed the case she'd prepared, placed notes for the kids in their rooms, and started to make her way out. I caught her in the garage. I snuck up on her and grabbed her, clamping a hand over her mouth so no one could hear her. But, she kept trying to scream, shout, and bite me as she kicked and fought back. I could barely hold on. She was so strong and desperate; it was almost an accident in the end. I'm not even sure if I meant to do it or not, given how much she fought. But whatever the case was, one moment she was alive and acting like some kind of wild beast as she tried to get away, and then, nothing. She just stopped. She went quiet and limp. She was floppy in my arms, a dead weight. I'd broken her neck. I can remember the noise. The sudden crack of bone. I think I was sick.

"I remember sitting there, looking at her on the floor, wondering what had happened. Then, sometime later, I'm not sure how long, but I realised the situation I was in. The kids were upstairs, asleep, and I'd just killed their mother. She was dead, and I'd done it. I panicked at first and dumped her in the boot of my car. I don't know how long it took me to come up with the plan, but at some point in the early hours, I drove out to Ranmore, found an empty car park, and dragged her into the woods as far off the beaten track as I could, and I buried her. I somehow got back to bed before the kids woke up, but I didn't sleep a wink."

"What did you do with her stuff?"

"I dumped it in a skip somewhere. I don't really remember where. It was somewhere random, anyway, and no one found it, so..." He shrugged.

"And then there was the police investigation," Jon said.

"I was in deep by then, up to my neck in it, so I just lied. That was easy. I've been lying to the police my entire life. I'm sure you're aware of my record."

"We are," Jon confirmed.

"I wanted to be there for my kids, but... I ended up failing them too. Jess more than Henry. I just... I saw Cathy in Jess. I saw Cathy's rebelliousness. I saw her fire, and I just didn't like what Jess was doing."

"Which was?" Jon asked.

"Modelling. Nothing seedy, not then. Not right away, anyway. That came later. But I still didn't like it. She never cared what I thought, though, and rightly so, I suppose. I think she was doing alright, last I checked."

"She was," Kate replied, "before she was killed."

Mickey grunted and returned his attention to the scarred tabletop.

His account of Cathy's death was sadder and less premeditated than Jon had thought it would be. Mickey actually sounded sad and remorseful about it. He seemed to realise that he'd made a terrible mistake and that he needed to atone in some way. It was not what he'd expected at all, but it all seemed to fit, and he had little reason to doubt him.

"So you're saying it was an accident?" Jon asked.

"It was. Yes. I didn't want to kill her. I just wanted to stop her from leaving me."

"As I'm sure you're aware, we're digging up the remains we found in the woods right now. They'll be tested and examined, so if you did break her neck, I think we'll know."

"Good." He didn't seem worried by the prospect, which only backed up his words.

"So, why not tell us about Jess?"

"Tell you what?" He looked genuinely confused.

"You killed her too, right?"

"What? No! No, I didn't kill Jess. I couldn't do that, ever. Cathy was a mistake. I've never killed anybody before or since. It was all just a big mistake. I did not kill Jessica."

23

"You're handling this well," Nathan said as they sped east, towards Leatherhead and hopefully a short search for Henry. "All things considered."

"What, you mean with all the craziness, like this mad woman who seems to have you all wrapped around her finger?" Ellie asked. "Or your history with a violent thug who's out for revenge?"

"Um, yeah, all that." When she put it like that, it all sounded a little insane, but somehow, it never did while he was dealing with it.

"Honestly, I'm just along for the ride at this point. I've got no idea where this is going to end up, but whatever. I'm having fun, and I'm sure it will work itself out in the end."

"I think you have more faith in us than is strictly warranted, but okay, I'll take that," Nathan replied.

"Do you think Terry, or Henry, or someone else is wrapped up in the murder of Jess?"

"Or dear old dad, Mickey, don't forget," Nathan added.

"Well, he's a career criminal as well, right. Like father like son."

"Yeah."

"So, he'll deny it. He'll be used to police interviews and just make up some sob story, making himself out to be the victim or something, get us thinking this is all a big misunderstanding. Whatever it is, he'll have a plan to try and minimise his role in Cathy's death and divert attention away from him."

"So, you think it's him?"

"Most murder victims are killed by those closest to them, right? So it stands to reason that Mickey or Henry are the most likely perpetrators."

"It does, which is one of the reasons to bring Henry in again and have another chat, in light of the new information we have."

"So, where are we headed?"

"Leatherhead. Henry is still listed as living with his dad, and we noticed that he was calling his dad's mobile all last night after we confiscated it."

"Maybe he's popped back home then, if he's wanting to speak to his dad."

Nathan held up a hand and crossed his fingers. "Here's hoping."

They pressed on, through the villages of Effingham and Bookham, before they turned off the bypass and made their way into Leatherhead, towards its one-way system as Nathan pondered how this might all play out. Was Mickey guilty? Ellie was probably right about him spinning a tale to make himself sound more sympathetic. From his record, it was clear he was used to dealing with the police and stressful situations in general, which would make him a tough nut to crack.

"So, what's the deal with Jon and this Ariadne woman?" Ellie asked. "There's something going on there."

"If there is, it's all coming from Ariadne's side. I'm convinced of that. For some reason that I cannot fathom, she seems very interested in Jon. I don't know why, but she is, and she seems to keep contacting him for some reason."

When it came to Ariadne, Jon played his cards close to his chest, and Nathan felt sure there was more that had happened between him and that woman than he was letting on. He didn't for one moment think he was cheating on Kate, but he was certain that Jon had run into Ariadne more times than Nathan knew about. How entangled was Jon with that woman? How compromised was he?

It wasn't a question he had an answer to, but Jon had always been a stoic, simple guy and didn't seem the type to either cheat or break the law. He trusted Jon and hoped he would always do the right thing.

"You're sure it's one-sided, that it's all coming from Ariadne?" Ellie asked.

"One hundred per cent."

"How can you be sure?"

"Because of Kate," Nathan stated simply. "She would not put up with any shit from Ariadne. I know that for certain. Jon however... I think things are a little more complicated there. I'm pretty sure I don't know everything that's going on, but..."

"He seems to be protecting her."

"I think he's actually protecting himself, and also the case. Reporting a mysterious woman who has a habit of showing up at our DCI's house, could be devastating to the case when it got to court. If that got out, it could get the whole thing thrown out, and the victims might not get the justice they deserve. I suppose there might be a little self-preservation in there, but what I *can* tell you, is that I trust Jon, and I believe he would always do the right thing. He's thinking of the victims and getting them justice."

Ellie sighed. "Yeah, sure. I can see that. I still think he's protecting her, though."

"I don't think so. If he found out that Ariadne was hurting innocents, I think you'd find Jon would be only too happy to throw her behind bars. As it is, she's stealing from the corrupt one-per-cent, the multi-millionaires who lead questionable lives, and I, for one, have no issue with that at all. Quite the opposite."

"And yet, back there, you were discussing a possible leak within the SIU? Meaning someone in the office is working for her? She might well steal from the corrupt, but her methods are dodgy as all hell."

"True. But Jon hasn't kept this suspected leak to himself. If he finds that leak, I think you'll find he plugs it."

"I hope so. I just don't like the idea that we're being spied on."

Nathan grimaced at the idea that everything about the case was being fed back to Ariadne. The idea made his skin crawl. "I agree, it's not a nice feeling, even if Ariadne's using it to help us, in her own unique way."

"Any idea who the leak is?"

"Nope. It could be any of us. I think it was happening on the previous case too."

"The missing boy one?"

"Yeah. That blogger we saw at the Lichwood house works for Ariadne too. That woman has her claws in everything."

"Hmm. Alright, so we're headed to Mickey's house, first, right?"

"That's right, and if we don't pick him up there, I have a list of other places we can search for him at." Although he hoped they wouldn't have to. He didn't really fancy the idea of traipsing around the local criminal underworld crack dens and hideouts, stirring up trouble while looking for this guy. But needs must, he guessed.

Pulling to a stop outside Mickey's house, Nathan scrutinised it with approving eyes. It was clean and well-tended, the opposite of many of the other houses on this road. Nathan wasted no time getting out and walking up to the front door. He was keen to move on if this first house turned out to be a bust.

After knocking on the door, Nathan stepped back to see what would happen. After a short time with no answer, he turned to leave, only for the front door to suddenly open and reveal Henry looking a little confused by the two strangers on his doorstep.

"Henry Thornton?" Nathan asked. Beside him, he noticed Ellie pull out her warrant card in preparation. She didn't show it, but she didn't need to. Henry caught sight of it, flicked his gaze back up to Nathan, and then bolted.

He turned and dashed into the house, disappearing from view.

"Here we go," Nathan griped as he hopped up the step and moved inside. Henry was already in the kitchen at the back of the house, where he quickly opened the back door.

"Shit," Nathan hissed and started running. "Police, stop where you are."

Predictably, he didn't listen, but he hadn't really expected him to. It was more of a courtesy than anything else. Fighting his way along the hallway, he charged through the kitchen and out into the garden at the back. Ahead, Henry was scrambling up and over a fence. Nathan grumbled internally at the idea of having to climb after him but pushed on anyway.

Seconds after he exited the narrow hallways and kitchen in the house, Ellie sprinted past him. Her younger, fitter legs helping to power her forward and start to close the gap. By the time Nathan reached the fence, Ellie was already swinging herself over the top and shouting after Henry.

With considerable effort, Nathan climbed up and pulled himself over, before dropping to the other side. He landed and ended up on the ground on all fours before getting up again. Ahead, Ellie vaulted over a shorter, waist-high fence, before she charged and tackled Henry from behind.

They fell out of sight.

Forcing himself on, Nathan ran to the next fence and saw Ellie wrestling with Henry on the ground. For a brief moment, he wished he had his taser on him, so he could pull it out and end this with a brief shock. But he knew he didn't have it on him. Instead, Nathan hopped over the second fence a little quicker and ran to help Ellie.

He might not be as young as he once was or as nimble, but he still worked out and could handle an unruly suspect. He also had a few tricks up his sleeve.

Within moments, he had Henry in an arm lock that rendered him useless and gave them control of the situation. Henry whined and protested, but they soon had him cuffed and cautioned before they walked him back to their car.

"You did well there, young un," Nathan said after closing the rear door on Henry.

"You too, old man."

"Touché. Let's get him back to the station and see what he has to say for himself."

24

"We'll call it a day there," Jon said before getting to his feet and stretching, allowing his blood to flow again. They'd been sitting in this room for a good portion of the morning, going over Mickey's story, picking it apart and teasing details out of him.

He was more forthcoming than Jon had any right to hope for, and it felt like they had a solid picture of what had happened the night of Cathy's disappearance. However, Mickey continued to assert that he had nothing to do with Jess's murder and would never have laid a hand on her, no matter what he thought of how she made a living.

And after he'd repeated the same assertation, over and over, Jon was even beginning to believe him. It didn't make much sense that he would admit to killing Cathy but refuse point-blank to admit to Jess's murder. Instead, he continued to say he believed a stalker was to blame.

Jon poured some ice-cold water on that idea, saying that their investigation had yet to find evidence that one of her known fans, or stalkers, was responsible. They were creepy and cruel, and guilty of bullying and harassment, sure, but murder? Probably not, based on the current evidence, although he couldn't really be sure.

In Jon's opinion, Ozzy was less likely to be the culprit due to the solid alibi. Ken, however, was less certain, and he'd yet to provide any kind of alibi. That, coupled with his pleasure room, made him more suspicious than Ozzy.

That wasn't to say there wouldn't be more of these so-called fans for them to talk to, though, and Dion was still going through Jess's messages, emails and social media. So who knew what was buried in there.

"Do you know where my son is?" Mickey asked.

"Henry? We've got some people out looking for him. He'll be brought in shortly. I think he deserves to know the truth, don't you? Besides, we have some questions for him."

Mickey frowned. "What's he got involved with now?"

"We can't discuss that," Jon replied.

"Okay, sure. Fine. But if you do bring him in, I'd like to see him, if that's possible?"

"I'll see what we can arrange."

Mickey gave him a nod and sat back, apparently satisfied.

"We'll tell him what happened with you."

"I know, that's fine."

Jon gathered his things and waited for Kate to do the same. Stepping out into the corridor, he spotted Nathan and Ellie talking quietly between themselves. "Back so soon?" he said, once Kate had closed the door.

"We found Henry. He's in there with a solicitor now." Nathan pointed to the room that was one up from where Mickey was.

"Well done. Where was he?"

"At his dad's. He ran for it when he saw us, but we chased him down."

"*You* chased him down?" Kate asked with a lopsided smile.

"Well..." Nathan stammered.

"I caught up with him and tackled him," Ellie clarified.

"That's more like it." Kate giggled.

"Hey, I'm not useless, you know," Nathan protested. "I caught up and helped subdue him."

"I'm glad you were made to feel useful, Grandpa," Kate said.

Nathan looked over at Jon and sighed. "Jesus, these young whipper-snappers, hey?"

"Oi! I'm thirty-six," Jon said in protest. "Hardly old."

Nathan grunted. "I'm surrounded by babes in arms."

Jon heard the door behind him and turned to see Mickey being led out by a uniformed officer. Their eyes met for a moment, and Mickey nodded to him before he was led away.

"How'd that go?" Nathan asked once Mickey was out of earshot.

"He admitted to killing Cathy, and burying her," Kate replied. "But he said it was an accident. He had hold of her from behind, his arms around her head and shoulders as he tried to keep her quiet, and in the struggle, broke her neck."

"Broke her neck?" Nathan sounded incredulous. "That's not easy to do."

"I knew it," Ellie commented. "I told you he'd find a way to make himself the victim, feed us a sob story."

"He could be telling the truth," Jon said.

"And he could be lying through his teeth," Nathan countered.

"Yeah, well, I guess we'll see. How long has Henry's solicitor been in there for?"

"Not long," Nathan answered.

"Right then, shall we go grab a coffee while we wait?"

"No need." Jon turned to the new voice. It was Ana Allen, one of their regular duty solicitors, leaning out from Henry's room. "He's happy to see you now."

Jon flashed a look at Kate and the others before looking back at Ana. "Thanks, we'll be right in."

"Okay," Ana replied and disappeared back inside.

"Are you going to talk to him about Terry?" Nathan asked.

"Absolutely."

"Mind if we watch along from the observation room?"

"Not at all," Jon replied. "Ready, Kate?"

"Sure, why not? Let's do this."

The four of them separated, with Nathan and Ellie making for the room at the end of the corridor, while Jon stepped up to the interview room and walked in with Kate close behind. Henry sat behind the table, still cuffed, looking annoyed as he slumped in his seat, his legs splayed apart, manspreading like a pro.

"Henry," Jon said in greeting. "Back again."

The young man gave a shrug that matched his defiant expression but said nothing.

Giving up on the possibility of a polite greeting, Jon took a seat and went about preparing for the interview in the usual ways, setting the recorder going and introducing everyone for its benefit.

Jon took a breath as he prepared himself to break the bad news to the young man about his father. He had little doubt that he would react badly, but he deserved to know, and there was a chance that it would create a small amount of trust or empathy between them.

"Thank you for coming in today, we do appreciate it," Jon started. "We wanted you in because we have a couple of things that we needed to discuss with you."

Jon paused, curious to see if Henry would say anything, but he didn't. Instead, the young man just stared at him and managed to look both bored and condescending at the same time. He decided to continue.

"Firstly, I think you need to know that we have your dad in custody."

"What!?" Henry snapped. He sat up, looking shocked and angry. "Why? What's he done? He didn't kill Jess."

Jon raised a hand, urging him to calm down. "We were watching your dad these past few days, and yesterday he drove out to Ranmore. We followed and discovered him digging up a body that had been buried in the ground for a while. We brought him in, and he's admitted to killing your mother, Cathy."

Henry's face fell as Jon revealed the sequence of events and the revelation that Mickey had killed Henry's mum. He looked utterly shell shocked, and after several seconds of staring at him and Kate, he looked away, his eyes searching the room. He attempted to form words and express himself, but nothing coherent came out.

Jon watched as the young man tried to process what he'd been told, and marry it up to what he knew as emotions crashed over him. He seemed lost.

"But, how... how can this..." Henry screwed his face up and gave his head a shake before he tried again. "He said she left. I thought she was alive."

"I'm sorry, but it doesn't look like it. We have people running tests on the remains, so we'll know for sure soon, but it does seem likely that this is your mother. Mickey admitted to it too. He volunteered the information, actually. I think he needed to tell someone."

"He believes it was an accident, though," Kate said. "She went to leave him in the middle of the night, after placing notes in yours and your sister's bedrooms, but he tried to stop her. It was during that struggle that he accidentally killed her."

Henry sighed and buried his head in his hands making the cuffs dig into his nose. "Oh god. I feel sick."

A moment later, Henry got up from the table and paced across the back of the room before coming to a stop at the right-hand wall and resting his head against it. "I got it so wrong," he muttered. "I always believed him, that she'd left us. That's what he told us, that she'd abandoned us. She said she'd be back in her letters, but I thought she was lying to soften the blow. But I guess she meant it. She would have come back, if he hadn't..."

"I'm sorry for your loss," Kate said.

"Please," Jon added, "if you wouldn't mind taking your seat again?"

"Could you be wrong?" Henry asked, sitting back down.

"When I found him in the woods, he was holding a shovel and was digging the body up. If the DNA tests prove that this is Cathy, then that along with your father's confession, pretty much seals it, and I don't see this going any other way, right now. I believe he'll be convicted for her murder."

"Jesus!" Henry took a moment to himself again as he sorted through his thoughts and emotions. Having experienced similar loss, Jon could make a guess at what his head was like, and knew the pain he would be in. After another few moments, which Jon was happy to grant him, Henry looked up. "So, are you saying that he killed Jess too?"

"No," Jon replied. "He categorically denies that. He says that he did not kill Jessica."

"Do you believe him?"

"That's not for me to say."

"I know but, I have to know. Do *you* think he killed her?"

"I... I don't think so, no, but I'm not the one that will need to be convinced, and while I might believe one thing or another, I have been wrong in the past. All we can do is collect the evidence. It'll be up to a jury to convict him."

"I know, I know. I just... I needed that. I needed to know what you thought."

"I understand."

"I just... I keep thinking back to that night, and all the times we've spoken about it through the years, thinking, did I miss something? Were there any clues? We've talked at length about this, about that night and what happened. Why didn't he tell me? He should have told me."

"He probably wanted to but couldn't find the words or the right time, I don't know. You'll have a chance to speak to him at some point, you can ask him those questions then."

"Okay, thank you."

"We still need to find the person who killed your sister, though."

"I understand."

"Do you have any idea who it might be?"

"No, not really?"

"You're sure?"

"Of course. I still think it was one of those sickos who follow her on that website. One of her fans. Did you look into them? She had some stalkers, I'm sure of it."

"We did yes, and there were two that stuck out above the others, but one has an alibi and the other... Well, we don't know. But there's nothing to tie him to the murder yet."

"I see."

"Were you aware of anyone else who might do this? Anyone at all? I only ask because, and don't take this the wrong way, but, we're aware of your criminal record and some of your known associates. Do you know anyone who might do this?"

"No, I have no idea."

"Are you sure?"

"Sure, I'm sure," Henry answered.

"Anyone you've worked with recently, perhaps? Someone you don't know the history of?"

"What are you getting at?"

"We have reason to believe that you're working with Terry Sims, Henry." Henry's reaction was immediate. His eyes snapped up, and he seemed to freeze in place.

"I thought so, I'll take that as confirmation," Jon said.

"No comment," Henry replied, making Jon's heart fall. Was he about to clam up now?

"Of course. Look, I understand that you've been through a lot today, but Terry is killing people. We have a source that tells us you're on his crew, and then we also have your reaction just now. But, we want to help you. After everything you've been through, I'd rather not put you behind bars, if possible."

In actuality, Jon was conflicted on this point. Losing someone close, to violence, is never easy. Henry had lost Jess a few days ago, and today he learnt that his mother was not alive and missing but was actually dead, killed by his own father, who would almost certainly be going to jail. Henry's life as he knew it was falling apart. If Henry was a model citizen they were informing of a death, they wouldn't be questioning him about alleged criminal associations, instead, they'd be offering counselling and support. Henry would get that same offer, but there was more to ask before they got there.

Jon felt sorry for him but also fervently believed that he should be locked up for what he'd done. Whichever way this played out, Henry would end up in the dock to answer for his crimes. But if he showed cooperation in light of recent events, a judge might go easy on him.

Henry didn't say anything. Instead, he preferred to stare at the wall, his mouth clamped firmly shut.

"Henry," Jon pressed on, "if you help us, if you answer a few questions, we can put in a good word for you with the judge if this goes to court. Show that you can work with us, help us, and you might get off lightly."

It was almost painful to suggest this to Henry, given his place on Terry's crew, but he had to remember, Terry was the bigger fish here. They needed to find him and stop him, and Henry might be the key to that.

Henry grunted.

Unsure how to take that reply, Jon forged ahead. "All I want to know is the answers to two questions. That's all. Just two. So let's take them one at a time, alright?"

Henry glanced at him but remained resolute for now.

"Okay. The first one's easy. Did anyone on Terry's crew know about your sister? Did they see any photos of her? Did they know about her profile on HoundPic? Was there any link between any of them and Jess? Anything at all?"

Henry sighed. He was a bright kid, and he was probably aware that if he answered that question in a certain way, he would basically be admitting to being on Terry's crew. But Jon couldn't help but remain hopeful that Henry's desire for justice for his sister would win out.

After a long moment, during which Jon waited with bated breath, Henry slowly looked up. "I don't think so."

"What don't you think?"

"I don't think anyone on the crew really knew her, not really. I can't be sure. I did swap a few messages with her before she was... you know. I possibly did say I had a sister to the others. We did talk about family and stuff, but they never met her. There was no link to her other than that."

"You're sure?"

"Well, no, not really," Henry said. "But nothing springs to mind."

"Did any of them see a picture of her?" Kate asked.

"Err, maybe. I don't know. I follow her on social media, so maybe, I guess."

"Do you remember any of them taking a particular interest in her?"

"No. I don't know, okay?" He sounded stressed. "I don't know."

"Okay, okay. In that case then, I only have one more question. Who's next on Terry's list?"

Henry stared at Jon.

"This is the big one, Henry. Answer this in a way that helps us, and I'll see what we can do to help you. But this is your moment. This is where you choose your future. All we need is a name."

"And if I don't know?"

"You know," Jon said. That question alone pretty much spelt it out for him. The kid knew who was next. He had to for them to plan the mission.

Henry let out another long sigh and hung his head for a moment as Jon waited. The whole room was on tenterhooks, as the tension in the room grew, as if the air itself was tightening.

"Victor Ackley," Henry said, glancing up. "He's going after Victor Ackley. In fact, they're probably already there."

"You mean, right now?"

"When Felix Miller disappeared, Terry said if anyone else was compromised, he'd need to adjust his schedule. He didn't exactly say how he'd adjust it, but given how desperate he was to exact his revenge..."

"He'd be worried about being stopped," Jon finished.

25

Jon had ended the interview right away, saying he would return to it later. For now, they needed to get to this Victor Ackley, whoever he was. They'd raced to the garage with Nathan and Ellie as Kate called up to Dion and got him to pull the details of Mr Ackley. By the time they were in the car, they had a full address punched into the sat nav as Jon pulled out onto the roads and headed north.

"We don't have much on Mr Ackley," Dion said over the phone that was set to the speaker and attached to the dash. "No criminal record, no links to crime of any kind. From what I can see, he's a very wealthy but very private man. He does a little charity work, but not much. And that's it, that's all I have for you, really."

"I've done a little research on him in my time," Nathan said over the conference call.

"What, why?" Jon asked.

"Because of who he is. I found some links to certain other wealthy men and women locally," Nathan explained.

"Might two of those be Elden Lichwood and Grey Davison?" Jon asked.

"They might," Nathan teased.

"Was this back during our investigation into the Black Hand and all that madness?" Kate asked.

"Before, actually. It was before you joined up when I was still hunting for clues as to what was going on, back when I was still a disgraced former DCI, and no one cared what I was doing with my time."

"Did you find out anything of note?"

"Not much, and it was a while ago, now. But like Dion just explained, he's a very private man, and other than some tenuous links to other more public men who we know of, there wasn't much to find out, not without running a much bigger and deeper investigation. It would have needed some undercover work and the backing of the higher-ups to run it. But I didn't have the reputation or evidence to do any of that."

"Well, Terry obviously thinks that Victor was involved if he's going after him."

"Obviously," Nathan agreed. He and Ellie were in the car behind, keeping pace with them.

"I've called in some backup for you, by the way," Dion said. "A firearms team and some patrol cars. They should be at the estate about the same time you arrive."

"Excellent, thank you, Dion."

"No problem, sir."

"Do we trust Henry enough to tell the truth?" Kate asked.

"I guess we'll find out, won't we," Jon replied. "I hope so. Otherwise we'll be giving this old man the fright of his life."

Kate smiled. "And won't that be fun?"

They raced north, passing under the M25 and through Cobham, their sirens and blue lights clearing the way and scaring a few of the morning shoppers. He hoped they'd be there in time to save Victor before Terry took his revenge. He had no idea if this next target was a criminal or not, but he probably didn't deserve to be killed. Very few people really did. After all, the criminal justice system was there for a reason, and it didn't do for people to drive around and deliver their own form of justice.

That kind of crap could get out of hand pretty quickly.

Dealing with Terry would be a relief. The man was causing problems and distracting him from Jess's murder investigation, which hung over Jon's head like the proverbial Sword of Damocles. He felt sure he was close to discovering who'd killed her. He could feel it in his bones that they were on the cusp of something but couldn't quite figure out what.

Maybe if they could remove Terry and his crap from the board, things might be clearer, and it might just throw up another suspect.

Who knew? Stranger things had happened.

Pushing north along the A307 towards Esher, they quickly followed the directions to the estate. Spotting the estate, surrounded by tall metal railings along the edge of the road, Jon turned off the lights and sirens, hoping to get the drop on them. With a quick order through the radio, the other cars did likewise.

Looking beyond the metal railings and trees, much deeper into the grounds, he saw a massive house that looked like it could home maybe fifty people? It would be better suited as a hotel rather than a private home.

Pulling in, Jon drove up to the open gates and eased his way inside, eyeing the guard's booth, but he couldn't see anyone in there. As he moved further in, Kate gasped.

"There, look," she said.

Jon turned and spotted the body laid out on the ground, half out of the guard post. At that moment, a marked police car turned in behind Nathan, and then another after that. Hitting the brake, Jon climbed out and waved at them before pointing to the body. One of the officers in the first car waved and pulled to the side onto the grass.

Satisfied that they would deal with the body, Jon got back in and raced towards the house. Beyond rises in the grounds in front of the building, he could make out a handful of vehicles parked out front, including a van, several saloons, and a black Lamborghini he'd seen before.

"Aaah, crap." That meant Ariadne was here.

"What?" Kate asked.

"She's here. Look. That black Lambo, it's hers."

"Hers? Oh, *hers*!"

"Yeah."

"Shit," Kate said through gritted teeth.

Racing to the wide driveway area before the house, Jon pulled up and jumped out. Already wearing his stab vest, he checked that Nathan, Ellie and the officers in the patrol car were following before pulling out his baton.

"Where's the firearms unit?" Jon called out to the uniforms.

"They'll be here soon," one of the officers replied. "We're armed, though."

Jon noticed the extra gear the two officers had, including the semi-automatic Glock 19M pistols strapped to the front of their vests.

"The men we suspect to be inside will be armed and dangerous," Jon warned. "They've already shot two men in the last few days."

"Copy that," the officer replied and pulled out his weapon. The second man did the same before they all advanced towards the house. As he passed the black Lamborghini, Jon noted the personalised number plate.

SP1D3R.

Yeah, Ariadne was here, alright.

Moving closer with the two armed officers, they approached the open front door. Just inside, another body lay on the floor, and he could hear voices. With a hand signal, he indicated they should hold for a moment, and listened in.

"Come on, we've got to go."

"Where's Lester?"

"He chased after that bitch, remember."

"Damn it, I knew I couldn't trust him. He's probably taken a fancy to her, hasn't he? Fuckin' pervert."

"Sir, let's go."

"Mel, Doug, we're leaving. Carl, check out front. I heard sirens earlier."

"On it."

The nearest officer glanced back at Jon, looking for permission to go. Jon gave a nod, and the two men ran inside.

"Police, drop your weapons."

Jon went to follow, but a gunshot rang out as he reached the door. He ducked as one of the officers fell to the floor. There was another shot. Jon looked up to see the thug closest, the one who'd shot first, also fall, shot by the second police officer.

"Hands up, freeze," the second officer ordered.

The wounded officer held his shoulder, bleeding through his fingers.

"Go on, get in there. I'm fine," the downed officer said.

Jon got to his feet and moved inside, with Kate close behind. Nathan and Ellie followed. The remaining officer had his gun trained on the man standing closest. He was bald, wore black, and still had a gun in his hand. He was also huge and well-muscled. Jon recognised him right away as Terry Sims from the photos he'd seen. Behind him, a man and a woman, also in black clothing, watched the confrontation with interest.

Jon recognised them too, as Mel Garner and Doug Turner, two of Terry's known associates.

"It's over Terry," Jon said. "You can't get out of this one."

"It's over when I say it's over," Terry rumbled.

"Not this time."

Terry grunted and looked past him. "Kate O'Connell, my-my, and Nathan! Well, I didn't think this would be a reunion. If I'd known you were coming, I'd have prepared a welcoming party."

"I bet you would," Nathan replied sarcastically.

"Drop your weapon," the armed officer repeated, but Terry just smiled.

As the officer spoke, Mel and Doug stepped closer, coming out from behind Terry and peering over.

Mel led the way. "Aww, it *is* Kate. Well, this is a turn up for the books. I've got a bone to pick with you. My leg hurts every day since you shot it. It's time I got some revenge."

"Absolutely," Doug added. Jon was well aware that Kate had shot both of these thugs when she'd been a part of the raid on Terry's hideout over a year ago. "I think we need to return the favour."

Jon looked between Terry and the two thugs, wondering where this was going, and hoping it wouldn't dissolve into a shooting match. Neither Mel nor Doug had a gun in their hands, but that didn't mean they weren't armed.

To his left, Kate stepped into Jon's peripheral vision holding a gun. She must have grabbed it from the wounded officer and was pointing it at Mel and Doug.

"Try it," Kate replied. "I need you both to get on your knees with your hands behind your heads, now."

"Don't be a fool, it's over, Terry," Jon repeated. "There's no way you can escape this."

Doug took a step closer. "Piss off."

To Jon's right, the officer adjusted his aim and pointed his gun at Doug.

Terry's arm snapped up. He fired.

The officer yelled and fell to the floor as Terry turned and ran. Kate fired once at Terry, but it went wide, missing him as he ran through a side door.

Jon cursed. He heard a yell to his right and saw Nathan locked in a hand-to-hand struggle with Doug. Mel pulled a gun, but Kate fired first and hit Mel's leg. The woman fell with a scream.

"You bitch," Mel yelled, dropping the gun. "Not my other leg."

"I've got the full set, now," Kate quipped as she kicked the gun away. "Don't move."

"Terry's getting away," Ellie hissed as she ran to the downed officer and checked him. The man moaned as Ellie checked the wound. "He's hit in the arm. He should survive."

"Go get him," Kate said, as Jon heard sirens approaching outside. "Ellie, go with him. I've got this."

"Kate, are you—"

"GO!"

Jon didn't need telling twice and bolted from the room, following Terry. He could hear Ellie right behind him, her feet pounding on the floor. Charging into an ornate living space, Jon spotted an old man lying still on the floor, a single gunshot wound to his head. Nearby was an open laptop, its screen glowing in the half-light.

He didn't slow and followed the sound of retreating footsteps, putting on a burst of speed.

"You're faster than Nathan," Ellie said from behind as she charged through another room.

"I doubt that's a high bar."

Ellie smirked.

Barrelling through a third room, Jon heard voices up ahead.

"What the hell are you doing." It was Terry, and he could hear yelps and cries that sounded female.

"Taking payment," replied another man's voice.

"You sick fuck," Terry spat.

Jon charged into the room, his baton ready. "Terry…" Jon trailed off as he took in the room. In the middle of another drawing-room, one of several he'd spotted so far, was a huge, ornate rug.

Laid on her back, Ariadne squirmed beneath Lester Harris, who held a knife to her throat as he struggled to pull his jeans down with his free hand.

They'd last seen Lester in the interview room suite at the station after Nathan and Ellie had finished interviewing him about Terry, and Jon recognised him right away.

Lester looked up in shock, blinked, and then smiled at them as he withdrew the blade. "Hi."

Ariadne briefly locked eyes with Jon and flushed with embarrassment. She twisted and kicked Lester off.

Taking advantage of the distraction, Terry fired at Ellie. She ducked and fired back. Both missed, but Terry was already running, and Ellie followed.

"Stop, or I shoot," Ellie yelled.

On the floor, Ariadne rolled away as Lester got to his feet.

He'd been trying to molest Ariadne, and Jon felt suddenly and intensely protective of her as a deep-seated, boiling rage flooded his mind. It wasn't a feeling he'd expected where Ariadne was concerned, but he went with it anyway. No one deserved to be raped, and there was no time for him to analyse his feelings now.

Lester lunged, slashing at Jon with his knife. The attack was clumsy and crude. Jon swung his baton and hit Lester's arm. He screamed, dropped the knife and fell to his knees.

A gunshot rang out. Jon looked up to see Ellie standing with her gun raised, and Terry on the floor halfway through a door. The man held his bleeding leg and hissed with pain.

"I got him," Ellie called out.

"Good job, watch him."

"He's not going anywhere."

A flash of movement to his right drew Jon's attention. Ariadne brandished Lester's knife and advanced on him as he knelt on the floor, holding his arm.

"Right, you little fuck," Ariadne hissed.

Jon grabbed her arm. "Don't. You're no better than he is if you do that."

Ripping her arm away, Ariadne glared at him. Her eyes were filled with rage and hate, all of it justified and understandable. But he couldn't let her stab, Lester. He needed to stand trial. For a moment, he thought she'd go through with it, but then her rage fizzled, and she dropped the knife.

"Fine, you're right."

Stepping back, he reached for his cuffs.

In a flash, Ariadne lunged and punched Lester in the face. He yelped and fell to the floor with a bloody nose.

Ariadne backed up, hissing with pain as she held the hand she'd hit him with, flexing her fingers. "Ow, that hurt."

"Done, now?" He gave Ariadne a look. "Feel better?"

"Much."

"Good."

Nearby, Terry laughed as Jon cuffed Lester. "Stupid fuck. He deserved that."

Jon raised an eyebrow as he finished securing Lester. Standing up, he approached Ariadne, who'd wandered off to the side of the room, still holding the hand she'd used to deliver the impressive punch.

"That's a mean right-hook you have there."

"Hmm, he's a twat."

"What happened?"

"Really?"

Jon gave her a look, suggesting he wanted to know.

"Huh. Okay, fine. He accosted me, threw me to the floor, and unless I'm very much mistaken, would have raped me… or tried to."

"And you're okay now?"

"Fine," she answered, although he didn't really believe her.

But, satisfied that she was basically unhurt, Jon changed the subject. "So, what the hell are you doing here?"

She grinned before answering, changing the pitch of her voice to something weaker and more vulnerable sounding. "I was here with Victor, in the middle of a business deal when these thugs just appeared out of nowhere. I ran for it, and this man chased me down."

Nearby, Terry laughed.

Jon shot him a look before turning back to Ariadne. He wasn't sure if he believed her or not.

"Alright." Jon had a feeling she wasn't being completely honest with him, but he was content to see how this played out. "Don't go anywhere."

"Wouldn't dream of it." She smiled demurely.

Firing her an incredulous look, Jon turned and walked over to Terry. Ellie had taken his gun and still had the one she'd taken from the armed officer trained on him. "You got him?"

"Oh yeah."

He turned his attention to Terry. "I told you we were done here."

"I'd have got away if it wasn't for that psycho." Terry nodded towards Lester. "I should have known he'd try something like this."

Jon frowned. "Why?"

Terry hissed as he held his bleeding leg. "Because he's done it before."

Jon looked around and spotted a tablecloth. He reached over and pulled it from the small ornate table, sending a couple of ornaments toppling. "Play nice, and I can tie off your leg with this."

Terry laid back. "Do it."

"Watch him," Jon said to Ellie, who adjusted her position for a better shot.

"You won't try anything silly, will you?" Ellie asked him.

"Wouldn't dream of it," Terry replied.

Jon set to work, wrapping the cloth around his leg above the bullet wound in his calf muscle. As he worked, he glanced up at Ellie.

"You're a good shot."

"I've done my firearms training," she answered with a smile, keeping her eyes on Terry.

"Good to know. I should do it myself sometime." Jon returned his attention to Terry. "So, tell me what Lester did before."

"He was on my crew after he got out, weeks ago. Thinks he's god's gift to women but constantly slags them off. He's a whiny mother fucker. But he's got some skills, so I get him some whores to keep him quiet. What's he do to repay me? He only goes and nearly kills one of them. Said she was slagging him off." Terry shrugged. "She was a bit of a mouthy cow, but she'd been paid, she would have fucked him. Bloody idiot."

Jon frowned and looked back at Lester, then at Ariadne, and then back at Terry as he started to see a pattern. "Do you think he would have done it? Do you think he would have killed the prostitute you saved?"

"Hell yeah. He'd already stabbed her when we caught him. She was screaming like crazy, and blood was everywhere. He was like a man possessed. I kicked him off the crew that night. I don't want that shit around me."

"And yet you brought him back," Jon mused as he glanced back at Lester.

"He had some skills that were... useful. Besides, I needed the manpower, especially after I lost Felix and Henry."

"Did Lester and Henry hang out?" Jon asked, turning back to Terry.

"Yeah. Hehehe. The sneaky fucker spotted Henry's sister on his phone this one time, so the next time Henry was fucked off his head on smack, he stole his phone and downloaded a few photos of her. Sick fuck. I'll bet he's been wanking off to them ever since. He bragged about what he'd do to her whenever Henry wasn't around. She's a looker, you know."

"She's also dead."

Terry frowned. "What?"

"She was murdered a couple of days ago. Stabbed to death."

"Well shit…" Terry shrugged. "Aaah well."

"You're being very cooperative," Jon remarked.

"Job's done mate. Job's done." Terry looked almost serene as he lay there. Jon pulled the improvised tourniquet tight, making Terry wince, before he grabbed Ellie's cuffs from her belt and secured his wrists.

He didn't resist.

With the threat reduced, Ellie relaxed, and Jon got to his feet. He turned and evaluated Lester as Kate ran into the room. She came to a stop just inside and surveyed the scene.

"Oh, what's all this?"

Jon wandered over. "Everything's under control here. Are you all okay?"

"We're fine. More backup arrived, so everything's secure." Kate noticed Ariadne and then looked back at Jon. "What happened?"

Jon turned and scowled at Lester. "I think we might have found Jess's killer."

26

"Based on what we now know, and according to all the evidence we've gathered, Lester Harris was the one who killed Jessica Thornton," Jon explained.

He was sitting in the Detectives Superintendent's office with Kate, Nathan and Ellie, after several long-winded interviews with a variety of people he'd not really want to spend any time in a locked room with. They'd picked apart Terry's, Lester's, Mickey's and Henry's statements, cross-checking and analysing everything, to build up a picture of the events surrounding Jess's murder and the deaths of Victor Ackley, Grey Davison and Elden Lichwood.

Some were very forthcoming and helpful, while others either refused to admit to what they were accusing them of or just outright refused to answer any questions at all, repeating the dreaded 'no comment' for hour after hour.

But what several of them were happy to do, especially when it came to Lester, was to snitch on him and make matters much worse for Jess's murderer. No one on Terry's crew seemed to have any loyalty to the man.

"Firstly, we have Lester's own criminal record. He was in jail for assaulting a woman and had already attacked several others before the one that got him sent down, so this wasn't his first rodeo."

"And we didn't detect this?" Superintendent Johnston asked.

"No," Nathan replied. "He wasn't a suspect in the Jessica case, and the tenuous connection didn't come up until well after we'd spoken to him. So there was no reason to suspect him."

"Then there's Terry's statement," Jon continued. "He seems more than happy to throw the man under the bus and says that while Lester was in his crew, he hurt a couple of prostitutes that Terry paid for. But there was one that he actually stabbed. He was also on the crew at the same time as Henry, although Henry didn't know about the attacks on the working girls.

"However, he does now remember Lester taking that interest, but what he wasn't aware of, was that Lester stole Henry's phone once while he was high on drugs and found out more information on her. He also downloaded some images of Jess, which we've found on Lester's phone. I don't know if he had her address from that little stunt, but I suppose it's possible. Henry does remember Lester's disgusting comments about women though and regrets not recognising the signs earlier. Anyway, we've also turned up a few more bits of corroborating evidence against Lester that are quite damning."

"Go on," the Super urged.

"Well, we knew that Jess went to a nightclub a few days before her murder, and we now have CCTV from that club that shows Lester talking to Jess. They weren't chatting long, and honestly, it looks like Jess wasn't enjoying his company and left. However, Lester followed, and we think he might have followed her home."

"But he didn't kill her that night?"

"No, he waited a few days first. We do now also have some security camera footage from the area that caught him passing by in the days leading up to her murder. And finally, and probably most damning, we have traces of Jess's DNA on the knife that Lester had on him in Victor's house."

"He did it then. He killed Jess. I think that's fairly conclusive."

"It's pretty solid," Jon replied. "But Lester refuses to admit it and claims he's innocent and a victim of circumstance."

"What about the woman at the house? The one he was attacking? What did she have to say?"

"Her name's Ariadne Silk." Jon didn't for one moment believe that was her real surname, probably not her real first name either, but that's what she gave to them as her name for the interviews. "She won't be pressing charges but did give an excellent account of the events in the house. According to her statement," and Jon wasn't sure how much of this to believe, "she was a close friend of Victor's and his sole remaining heir. She was there as a friend, and to do some business with him, when Terry and his crew attacked. She ran, and Lester chased her down."

Jon, however, didn't like this explanation at all. Her presence at this murder was far too suspicious, and convenient. Was she working with Terry? He wasn't sure about that either. He wasn't her style. But, she had to have known what was going on, and planned to take advantage of it somehow.

Whatever the truth was, she seemed innocent to a casual observer, and Terry's crew backed up her statement to the letter.

"She's going to be a very rich woman," Johnston commented.

"She already was, but yes."

"Why did Terry allow Lester onto his crew if he knew what kind of man he was?"

"Terry's been kind of vague about that. He's mentioned some skills that Lester has that were useful, but it was also because of the pressure that we put on him and his crew. Somehow, probably through the lure of money, Terry got a Miller on his team. When word got back to the Millers that

Felix Miller was working with Terry—an old enemy of the family—they pulled him back in. Between that and us bringing Henry in, it forced Terry's hand, and Lester was the only man he could get at short notice."

"Ok, good work. And we have Henry's father, Mickey, in for a six-year-old murder of his wife, right?" Johnston asked.

"That's right, sir. He's admitted to it."

"Alright. Nathan, how're things coming with the case against Terry?"

"He's denying involvement, naturally, and we know the lawyer he's got is one of the most prestigious in the country. Ridiculously expensive and well connected. So I don't know how that will go. We have incredibly solid evidence, though, so we'll do our best. We know he did it. He killed those three men."

"I have faith in you, Nathan. Bring it home."

"I'll try."

"And Ellie," Johnston said, turning to her, "how was this experience for you? Do you think you'll be sticking with us for a while?"

"It was great, thank you, sir. It's been a real pleasure to work with Nathan, Kate and DCI Pilgrim. I've learnt a lot. I've enjoyed myself and got a lot out of the whole experience here. So, if it's alright with you, I'd very much like to stay on the team."

"Excellent. Happy to have you," Johnston replied with a comforting smile. "I've been very impressed with your performance."

"Thank you, sir."

"Alright then, you lot. I've got work to do, so off you go."

"Sir." Jon got to his feet and led the others out of the superintendent's office and back into the main open-plan area.

Once they were a distance away from the office, he turned and offered his hand to Ellie.

"Well done in there. I'm thrilled to have you on the team, keeping Nathan in line. He can be a bit of a troublemaker, sometimes."

"I'll keep him in line as much as I can."

"Thanks. And Nathan, Amazing work as always. I know those higher up might never formally recognise the work you've done against that hidden organisation, but you've certainly proved yourself to me. I don't know how long it will take, but I promise I'll get you back up to your former rank of DCI as soon as I can."

"Cheers guv." Nathan turned and led Ellie away with a wave of his hand.

"No problem."

"And now the real work begins," Kate grumbled, no doubt thinking about the stacks of paperwork they had to prepare for the court battles to come.

"It certainly does," Jon agreed.

"I'd like to have a chat with you later," Kate said.

"Oh, what about?"

"Sir?" said a voice.

Jon looked up at the interruption. It was Debbie Constable walking over to him. "Yep, what's up?"

"I have Miss Silk downstairs. She said she'd like to see you."

"Oh," Jon said, his stomach sinking. He thought she'd left already and shot a concerned glance at Kate. What on earth did that woman want now? But as he thought about it, he remembered something. Something had occurred to him during the interviews with her, but he never got a moment alone with her to bring it up. Maybe he'd have an opportunity to now. "Okay, I'll come down."

"I'll go with you," Kate said. Jon nodded, quite happy to have her along as backup.

Debbie turned to her, her eyes tick-tocking between them. "Um, she said only Jon."

"All the more reason I should be there," Kate replied.

"Oh, okay," Debbie stammered, sounding unsure. But she turned and led them out of the office to the stairwell.

"How's your son?" Kate asked her.

"He's okay," Debbie answered. "He's with his dad today."

"Oh, okay. Sorry to hear about your separation. Are you alright?"

"I'm fine," Debbie answered. "It was tough at first, downsizing like that, but we get by as best we can."

"Let me know if I can help," Kate said.

"Can I work less hours for more money?" Debbie sent a cheeky smile back at them.

Jon grimaced at the comment, understanding that she had it tough and that the pay wasn't amazing for a civilian investigator. It wasn't terrible either. But as a single mother, he could only imagine how hard it was for her.

"Let me see what I can do for you," Jon replied.

Debbie smiled. "Thanks."

She led them out towards the reception area and into a side room, where Ariadne was sitting. As Jon entered the room, she got to her feet and swanned over, swinging her hips. She'd regained her composure and poise since her ordeal at the mansion.

"Jon." She smiled, but it faded when she saw Kate follow him in. "And the lovely Miss O'Connell."

"I'll be outside," Debbie said and stepped out, closing the door.

"We're even now," he said the instant the door closed. He felt relieved to get it off his chest after coming to the realisation hours earlier. There was no point in indulging in polite conversation or giving her any chance to beguile him with her words. He wanted to take control and tell her how things were going to be.

"What?"

"You saved my life and helped with the case. I just saved your life and saved you from being raped. I think that makes us even, don't you?"

Ariadne frowned and pursed her lips as she considered the point. But then shrugged and smiled sweetly. "Sure, why not. Consider us even."

"Good." Jon smiled, pleased with himself. "So why did you want to see me?"

"Oh, just to say goodbye. That's all. It's been fun."

"Goodbye?"

"I'm heading for pastures new, Jon. I've had fun here, with you and your little friends, but I think I'd like some new challenges."

"Okay," Jon replied, feeling a sense of relief, as if a weight had been lifted off his shoulders. "Great."

"I'll miss you, and our little chats."

"I wish I could say the same, but..."

"Cute." She lowered her face and peered up at him with sultry hooded eyes. Her voice lowered with a husky tone. "Maybe we'll run into one another again one day."

"I sincerely hope not."

"Not if I can help it," Kate added. "Besides, I'll be moving in with Jon soon, so you'll have me to deal with if you do show up."

Jon gave her a shocked look but hid it quickly. He'd not expected to find out like this. Had she really just said she was moving in with him? Had she made up her mind already?

"And won't that be fun," Ariadne replied, her words dripping with sarcasm.

"Not really," Kate said.

"Well, if we're all done here, I think I'll leave you to your mountains of paperwork." Ariadne made for the exit and gave them a little wave before disappearing through the door. "Adieu."

And with that, she was gone.

Jon watched the door for a moment, half wondering if the woman might suddenly reappear with another smart comment. But she didn't, and the room was left in silence. Jon turned to Kate. "So, do you want to move in with me?"

"Is this what you wanted to talk about?"

"Yeah," Jon admitted.

"Okay, well, if you'll have me?"

"Well, yeah, of course. I'd love to. But, only if you want to. You don't need to."

"I want to," she replied and stepped closer, wrapping her arms around his neck. "It'll be a new chapter. It'll be fun."

"It will." He gave her a kiss. "Right, well, it looks like we've got a lot of work to do. Let's get to it."

***

Debbie turned as the door opened, and Ariadne stepped out of the side room, leaving Jon and Kate inside. She smiled at the woman. "Shall I see you out?"

"Please," Ariadne replied and strode confidently across the reception. As they passed the front desk, Debbie grabbed the signing in book, and sped up to catch Ariadne.

"Um, you need to sign out."

The raven-haired woman turned and glanced once at the book. "Pen?"

"Here." Debbie passed her one.

She watched as Ariadne scrawled her name on the ledger and handed the pen back. She went to turn away but stopped and leant in, speaking in low tones. "Thank you for all your help, Mrs Constable. Or is it Miss now?"

"We're still married, for now."

"Of course, these things take time. Let me know if you need help with all that. And, thank you. Your 'help' was invaluable. If it wasn't for you, none of this would have been possible. I would keep an eye on your bank account if I were you."

"Oh, okay." Debbie felt a rush of excitement flush through her body at the hint of more money. Making that phone call and telling her about the case had felt like a betrayal of Jon, Kate, and the whole SIU, but Ariadne's offer had just been too tempting.

"Suffice to say, we're done."

"I understand." Relief flooded through her, hoping Ariadne wouldn't want anything else out of her.

"Unless I return, one day. Who knows..." Ariadne bobbed her eyebrows at her. "Keep out of trouble."

Debbie swallowed as the tension returned, and Ariadne stalked out of the building. She turned and saw Jon and Kate exit the room. They smiled and waved. Debbie waved back as she heard the roar of Ariadne's car in the distance.

"Back to work," she said to herself and headed upstairs.

THE END

I'm starting a new British Crime Thriller series.

The Sherwood Forest Murders

follows Detective Loxley, Jon Pilgrims former colleague, as he hunts down a cruel killer in Nottinghamshire, Jon's former constabulary.

Book 1 of the Nottinghamshire Crime Thriller series

Available here:

www.amazon.co.uk/dp/B09R84QQ28

Author Note

Thank you for reading this sixth book in the DCI Pilgrim series. I really appreciate it. These six books have been amazingly fun to write, and I am thrilled that they have been so well received by readers like yourself.

You may have noticed that I wrapped up a few story threads in this book, and that was done on purpose.

I won't say this is the last ever Pilgrim book, but I do want to try a new Crime Thriller series.

I've already, mentioned it on the previous page, and this new series will be A Nottinghamshire Crime Thriller series, and begins with The Sherwood Forest Murders.

The series will follow Detective Loxley as he takes on a deadly new case.

You might have noticed Loxley's name earlier in this book, and that's because Rob Loxley is Jon's former colleague and team member.

Who knows, maybe Pilgrim and Kate will show up as well at some point.

Wink

Anyway, I hope you will join me in the new series which will be released in a few months.

You can order it here:
www.amazon.co.uk/dp/B09R84QQ28

In the meantime, thank you once again.

Kindest Regards,
A L Fraine.

www.alfraineauthor.co.uk